Praise for the ...

"Bhavna's last words become strength for Ajay, who lives to fulfill his promise of love."

— *Business Standard*

"... channelise his agony into writing. The result? Two best-selling novels, *You Are the Best Wife* and *Her Last Wish*, based on a true love story.

— *The Asian Age*

"... a semi-autobiographical book on vanquishing loneliness."

— *Mid-Day*

"... anyone who is going through a rough phase in terms of a personal relationship must read this."

— *Deccan Chronicle*

"... Pandey beat the likes of JK Rowling and Devdutt Pattanaik to go to the top of the bestselling list in India."

— *Mid-Day*

"...Ajay K Pandey hit the big league of pulpy romance"

— *Quartz India*

"... a bestselling book is made"

— *Scroll.in*

"The real love story will pull you in a pool of emotions."

— *Jagran*

"There are some books that are not just stories but reflection of realiti... ...wife is one such book.

— *WritersMelon*

"The Indian author has given reasons to believe that India has not only given good tech-heads, but are delivering literary moths too."

— The Truth India

"The loving heart of a beautiful soul Bhavna, encouraged Ajay to fight back and start looking at life in a positive way."

— India Café 24

"It is one of the purest, heart-warming love stories I ever read..."

— Salisonline.in

You are
the Best Wife

a true love story

Ajay K Pandey

Srishti
PUBLISHERS & DISTRIBUTORS

SRISHTI PUBLISHERS & DISTRIBUTORS
Registered Office: N-16, C.R. Park
New Delhi – 110 019
Corporate Office: 212A, Peacock Lane
Shahpur Jat, New Delhi – 110 049
editorial@srishtipublishers.com

First published by
Srishti Publishers & Distributors in 2015

Copyright © Ajay K Pandey, 2015

30

This is a true story. The author has tried to recreate events, locales and conversations from his memories. He may have changed some identifying characters and details such as physical properties, timings, occupations, dialogues and places of residence of people mentioned herein.

The author asserts the moral right to be identified as the author of this work.

Printed and bound in India

Dedicated to Bhavna's parents.

*I will always be thankful to both of you for
blessing me with such a loving wife.*

There are two kinds of personalities. There are those who have everything and still complain as if they have nothing. And there are those who lose everything and act like life has given them everything. Sometimes both these personalities exist in the same soul. Kill the first one, I love the second.

–Bhavna

Prologue

28 November 2012
Fortis Hospital, Noida

Those memories still send a sharp, stinging pain through me. I walked to the Fortis internal medicine ICU. My heart was racing and I was flooded with emotions. After a few minutes, I was standing outside the ICU door; Bhavna was behind a green curtain.

"Listen, you have to be brave and calm. I want to inform you that Bhavna's condition is deteriorating further and we're planning to put her on a ventilator," the doctor said in a concerned tone and handed me a document to sign.

I felt numbed. As these icy words pierced me, it felt as if my blood was freezing.

"What are the chances of recovery?" I asked bluntly.

"Rare chance; once she is doing well we can remove her from that, but her condition is getting worse. The ventilator is not the problem, the infection is."

"So, is she not on ventilator yet?" I asked. "Can I see her?"

"That is what I called you for. This ventilator will only be removed once she starts recovering or there are signs of improvement. She'll be administered anesthesia which will make her unconscious so that the ventilator doesn't cause any damage."

"What if there are no signs of improvement?" I asked.

"Then, I'm sorry..." he sighed. "It is possible you'll be talking to her for the last time."

I went behind the green curtain. I thought I would hug her, but that would make her feel that something was wrong and she might break down completely. With a heavy heart and this dilemma in mind, I went to her. There was blood around her lips. She lay with her mouth open and her eyes closed. It was the most horrifying moment of my life. Watching her struggle to breathe made me insane. I wished I could have given her my breath and a part of my life, but I was helpless. I had never felt so disabled in my life.

With great difficulty I said, "I love you, Bhavna. And you are the best wife."

She collected her strength and whispered something with ragged breaths.

My life changed from that day onwards. What my life was before and what it became after, is something that forced me to write this book. I wish I could rewind time and go back and relive all the beautiful moments that we had cherished together.

Ragging is a Criminal Offence

There are three kinds of students: ones who are sure what they want and achieve it, ones who know what they want but never achieve it, and finally (the kind that I am) those who don't know what they want.

After completing my schooling from Rihand Nagar, Sonebhadra, UP, I was like all the others who took the age old path of engineering. There was no decision making involved in the choice; those who took maths would appear for the engineering exams, so I too joined the rat race.

I joined a coaching class for the IIT entrance exam. I wasted two years in the hope of gaining admission into an IIT. Being a brahmin by birth, I had always prayed to God at the top of my voice, considering him deaf. This time, the prayers were centred on just one thing.

"God, please let it be IIT, please let it be IIT."

Sadly, IIT and IERT sounded alike to God and in this confusion, he gifted me IERT. It seemed as though God used BSNL operator services, which go down during the rainy seasons, and with the sounds of thunder around him, God heard IERT instead of IIT.

And so I landed up at IERT and finally realized that it was what I wanted. Nevertheless, I was not disheartened and accepted the same with love and respect. I was full of respect because when all the colleges had shut their doors, only IERT had accepted me.

August 2003
IERT (Institute of Engineering and Rural Technology) Allahabad

I joined the IERT hostel on the second day of college and my father and I both received a warm welcome from the hostel warden at the reception.

"Welcome to one of the finest engineering colleges in the country," he said with a sense of pride and achievement.

I looked at my father; his chest had swelled with pride at the warden's warm welcome. My father and Sachin Tendulkar suffered from a similar disease: the 'nervous nineties'. But in my father's case, it was his weight that was always swinging between ninety and ninety-nine kilos. He certainly scored a century then as he watched his son entering the Rural Technology Institute. I was the first in the Pandey family to study engineering. My father had another reason to be happy. Finally, I had got admission into a college, which would mean an end to money grubbing by coaching institutes.

"Sir, is ragging a big problem for freshers?" my father asked the warden, concerned.

"Pandeyji, you don't have to worry as the Supreme Court has declared ragging as a criminal offence."

The manner in which he had said this seemed to indicate that he was personally in touch with the Supreme Court judge who gave the verdict.

"Are the seniors staying in the same campus?" Papa asked in the same concerned tone.

"Yes, but their building is a different one," the warden answered.

After sometime, when Papa had settled me into my hostel room, I sensed one of his 'gyaan sessions' was about to start.

"Sonu, you have to study seriously. You are at a very crucial juncture of life, as you have to handle everything by yourself from now onwards. No cigarettes, no alcohol, no bad company, and no girlfriends! We belong to a middle class family, and you are our only hope."

He sighed.

Sonu is my nickname. I was surprised by my father's remarks. He had never had an opportunity to study at a professional institute. His words made me feel emotional but at the same time I felt overburdened by my family sins. Suddenly, I didn't know why my hopeless family was searching for hope through me.

"Ok Papa," I nodded, although I knew I would not follow any of his instructions. But I said this to stop him from repeating his old refrain. That day however, he was unstoppable.

"Now all the family glory is in your hands and lastly...," I felt relieved on hearing the word 'lastly' from him, '...Remember, beta, you are my brave son."

With those inspiring words, he left for Rihand Nagar.

His last words bewildered me. Why would he call me his brave son?

❖

That evening at around eleven, I entered the common room to find many new faces. I met Arvind.

"Hi, I'm Arvind Chaubey, computer science. I'm from Rihand."

"Hello buddy, I am Ajay. In electronics, from Rihand Nagar, NTPC colony," I replied.

Arvind frowned, "Just Ajay?"

"Oh, it's Ajay Pandey."

In a place like Allahabad, surnames matter a lot. People may forget your first name, but not your surname. We both exchanged a half-hug, or to be more precise, a manly hug. The sense of belonging to the same place seemed to have brought us closer instantly.

Before I go on, let me introduce all my hostel friends since their names will come up time and again:

Arvind Chaubey: We both came from the same town. He was a simple, but often irrational man. Love and girls were all Greek to him. He was heavy set and we thought of him as a clone of Salman Khan.

Gaurav Singh: My roommate. He was cheerful, talkative, confident and confused at the same time. No one dared to talk to him as it meant only listening from the other side.

Dipendra Singh: I hate to say it but, he had been my junior at take to next line St Joseph's School and he was a master at analyzing girls. I can't even bear to mention the kind of things he would find out about them, things Google itself would fail at. He was a master at talking to girls with no hesitation. Sometimes, I felt he might have committed suicide if IERT was a 'boys only' institute. He was almost six feet tall, thin, smart and, yes, handsome, too. Because of him, I realized that looks matter a lot.

Sorry friends, but that is my description of you guys. If any of you are going to file a case against me, please remember: all the above characters are fictitious. Any resemblance to real persons, living or dead, is purely coincidental. Now I'm free to tear your undergarments, but you know the truth – I love you all.

At 11:30 p.m., I was lying in my boxers and was about to fall off to sleep. Suddenly, a group of half a dozen gregarious men started pounding heavily on every door, shouting like military men.

"Everyone assemble in the corridors! Move! Now!"

The shouting was quite scary, but seeing everyone moving towards the corridor, I followed. We stood lining the walls of the corridor while the seniors stayed in the middle. They seemed like dacoits and we shivered like poor villagers.

"Third button! No eye contact!" one senior shouted at me. I hung my head like a war prisoner.

The introduction had a set pattern: full name, branch, and place of origin. We did this in a flash. Then, one senior shouted in a horrible voice.

"Lights off," he instructed one of his friends. I was a bit at ease and I raised my head a little, but it was just the calm before the storm.

"Remove all your clothes," one senior shouted.

Everyone, including Gaurav, took off their clothes. I could make out their nude bodies even in the dim light. I could have never imagined such a sight even in my wildest dreams. Now I understood why my father had called me his brave son.

They switched the lights back on. Manav Bahadur and I were not a part of the exhibition, yet. We were still wearing our boxers since we had joined on the second day of the ragging.

"Do you need a special invitation?" One senior shouted at Manav.

"It is not possible, sir," Manav said.

Five seniors jumped on him and forcefully took off his boxers. They started swinging his boxers in the air with pride, their laughter echoed in the corridors and our ears. A rape scene from an eighties Hindi movie flashed across my mind. By the time they had turned to me, I had taken off my boxers and was standing nude, hiding my family jewels with my palms.

Manav's dark ass had also joined the group of nude freshers. I mentally pleaded with all the known gods, hoping at least one would listen. *My turn*, I thought. I was once again reminded of my father's words, *our family glory is in your hands*.

I thought to myself, *I don't know about the family, but yes, my glory is in my hands*.

"Give your introduction, again!" A senior shouted.

"Ajay Pandey, Electronics from..." I was interrupted.

"Landey, he is also a Pandey. Handle him," the senior said while looking at one of the half dozen seniors. A creature with dark brown eyes and dozens of pimples on his face approached me. I had guessed his name was also Pandey. I was in a state of shock. *What if tomorrow my classmates start calling me Landey?*

While I was busy mulling over *Pandey* versus *Landey*, he neared me and started touching my chest. As his fingers inched towards my glory, I pleaded *Oh God, please don't let him be gay! And please have mercy! Hope he belongs to the same caste.*

"Please, Pandey sir," I begged. Thankfully the Pandey saga worked and he released me.

One senior shouted, "Juniors raise your hands." We obeyed; now our glory was visible to everyone.

I learnt a very important fact that day: one's glory is inversely proportional to one's build.

"Juniors, you have to scream in unison, '*Hammam me sabhi nange hain.* We were all nude'."

I was puzzled but consulted with Gaurav who was standing very close to me. "What is 'Hammam'?" I whispered.

"Shhh! 'Hammam' means bathroom," he whispered back.

I felt humiliated again, but we shouted, with our glory hanging and our hands in the air.

"Hammam main sabhi nange hain."

It felt like we were provoking the enemy.

"Listen juniors. Yesterday, we explained the rules and today we are adding some more. No one is allowed to close their room doors before 2.00 a.m. Till then, you have to wear formal shirts and pants. No casuals are allowed. Whenever any senior calls you, you have to be as quick as a tiger and form a queue."

What crazy people! First they want us to behave like tigers and then like sheep, I thought to myself.

"Today we're leaving you a bit early because tomorrow you have to report thirty minutes earlier for class at 8:30 a.m. You have to grab a seat right behind the girl you like the most. She'll be your *'maal'* for the future and the rest of the hostellers will help you. If there is any confusion or conflict of interest, bring it to our notice and we'll resolve the same. Understand punks, day scholars should not have access to any maal, they should belong to the hostellers."

We smiled mischievously. Only the word 'maal' could make us smile in such a terrible nude state.

"Any doubt, juniors?" One senior questioned.

"When will the ragging end?" Manav asked.

A senior came to Manav and caught his neck shouting, "This is ragging? You think this is ragging?"

"Explain to him why this is not ragging!"

The seniors pulled at Gaurav, but he remained silent.

"Listen, juniors, this is not ragging! It is training! We're training you to make you stronger and smarter, and the training will end after the freshers' party."

His philosophy went over our heads. I was about to faint.

"Dress fast and start using deodorants," the same senior screamed, covering his nostrils. "You guys are really rustic. Please make sure that you are clean shaven from now on," he added, "including your faces."

❖

Gaurav and I both settled into our room. I checked my watch; it was 1.00 a.m.

"This is early? Are they idiots?" I cried in frustration.

"What happened?"

"It's one o'clock at night and this is early for them! Moreover, we have to reach before nine tomorrow and choose a 'maal'! Is this what we have come here for?" I shouted but Gaurav kept silent.

He ignored my questions and sank into his bed.

I closed my eyes and lay on my own bed, missing my school days and school crush, Ragini. Her short, cute hairstyle and smiling face were running through my mind. But when you are going through a tough time, even your roommate will add salt to your wounds. Gaurav jumped on to my bed.

"What happened?" I asked, scared, wondering if he was also interested in taking my glory away from me.

"Yaar, Manav's nude, black ass is flashing in front of my eyes."

"So?"

"So, I can't sleep. Please help me lighten up with a joke, so that a bit of today's humiliation can be forgotten."

Now I understood why a talkative person like him was silent. It was damned Manav's black ass!

"You want me to crack a joke at one at night?" I asked in frustration.

He nodded, and said, "Please."

I thought for seconds and said, "You know the biggest joke at IERT? Ragging is a criminal offence." We laughed.

My First Interaction
with Bhavna

My first day at college was horrible. After the late night humiliation, I woke early in the morning and reached the assigned section 'A'. The letter 'A' and the word 'morning' always excites me because all the movie halls run Grade A shows in the morning. But this day was different.

At around 9:05 a.m., girls started entering the classroom in small groups. *Why do girls always remain in groups?* I thought. Maybe because girls are fewer in number, and minorities always feel more secure in homogeneous groups.

Like all other engineering colleges, there were fewer girls than boys in the class. They could all be accommodated in one row.

In Allahabad and at the IERT, girls and boys sit apart. It felt like India and Pakistan. No one was allowed to cross the LOC. As instructed, all hostellers had settled down in the second row. We were yawning; mouths open wide like crocodiles and water running from our eyes with every yawn.

I settled in between Arvind and Dipendra, in the wild hope of getting some eye tonic. It would help us recover from the restlessness due to our lack of sleep. My jaw dropped on seeing the terrible dress code. All the girls looked like pathans; covered from top to bottom in grey kurtis and dark grey salwars, their chest enveloped by snake-like dupattas. I noticed that their hair was tied back with red ribbons. It reminded me of the model in the government advertisements for the Shaksharta Mission.

"Welcome to rural technology, Ajay," Arvind whispered. I frowned and realized, two cunning friends always think alike.

Soon someone informed me that one of the rules of ragging was that the girls had to wear red ribbons. It was a great relief to know we were not alone in our misery. The girls were also undergoing similar humiliation. At least ragging does not have any gender bias.

The girls settled in the first row. A beautiful girl was sitting diagonally across to me. Surprisingly, she was not wearing a red ribbon which caught my attention.

She had short hair so she could not tie it back with ribbons. She had used at least half a dozen of clips to keep her hair from getting frizzy. Her short hair reminded me of Ragini. My mind had committed the cardinal sin of comparing two girls. *This new girl seems to be more beautiful than Ragini*. But my daydream was interrupted.

"Good morning, sir," everyone screamed in unison.

"Good morning, students," the professor replied.

A towering six-and-a-half foot professor with a pot belly and curly hair entered with a fake killer smile. With his heavy build and canvas shoes, Professor Bisht looked like a sports teacher.

He started to take attendance. Because no one knew their roll numbers yet, he started calling out our names. After fifteen names had been called out, he said the name Bhavna and the short-haired girl responded, "Yes, sir".

She looked stylish, wearing spectacles that complemented her beauty like accessories would. Those spectacles made her look like a doctor. A smart doctor. She was smart but that does not mean she was not beautiful. I only want to imply that she was so smart that her beautiful looks were overshadowed by her smartness.

After fifteen minutes of a slow poisonous attendance round, Bisht sir wrote 'Electrical Engineering' on the board with a white chalk. It took him five minutes to draw circular orbits. He jabbed five times at a single point on the outer orbit with the piece of white chalk. An inch broke off his three inch piece of chalk and fell to the ground like a bomb. The electron he had drawn ended up looking like a spider stuck in its own web.

No one in the world could stop me from falling asleep in the face of the professor's sluggishness. All the other hostellers were suffering in the same manner as they tried to keep themselves conscious. Our eyes watered with each yawn.

Contrary to his physique, Mr Bisht's voice was very thin; it was like the dacoit Gabbar Singh speaking with the voice of a bubbly twelve-year-old girl. We glanced at each other and smiled mischievously. Mr Bisht noticed this and stopped teaching abruptly, not uttering a single word. A deadly silence followed. Even the snails stopped crawling. He glared at us furiously. After a few seconds of silence, he flared his nostrils.

"Dear students, please try to understand if my blood boils, then you are not going to cook rice over it. That boiling blood will definitely harm you lethally."

Everyone burst out laughing. The short-haired girl also smiled, and her cheeks dimpled.

What a great smile! I became an instant fan of her smile. I snapped myself out of it and putting a hand on my chest, mumbled, "Mr Ajay, please stay within your limits. You should not develop another crush."

❖

In the hostel, after dinner at around ten, as expected the moronic seniors returned. Our glory was at stake again but we did not feel embarrassed today. Maybe we were getting used to it. Because it was true that *'hammam me sabhi nange the'*. We were all nude. We had assembled in the corridor again, with our glory hanging loose. The seniors began taunting us again.

No, no more, I prayed to the Almighty.

Perhaps the congestion in God's network superseded, and no one intervened with any help.

"Juniors, tell us the name of your targets. Hopefully you have chosen the one."

"Akansha Singh." As expected, Dipendra shouted first.

"Beena Mishra," Arvind said.

"Parul Tripathi," Gaurav said with a cunning smile on his face. His smile reflected the seriousness of his thoughts.

I was amazed to hear that these girls were in my class. Where were they? Why hadn't I seen them? Finally, it was my turn.

"Bhavna," I said. I had only noticed her.

"Oye, hero! What's her full name?" One senior shouted at me.

I was stuck and started looking for help anxiously. Dipendra jumped in as a saviour. "Bhavna...Pradhan."

As expected, Dipendra was more aware about girls than anyone else present there. The senior left with this last commanding announcement.

"Juniors! You can be asked about your target at any time, so start paying attention." That night, they ended their so called training at around two.

❖

We had Graphics lab after a few days. Laboratory classes in Engineering were an opportunity for students to spend time together for three hours. The boys could flirt with their targeted ones during the time.

In order to accomplish my ragging task, I'd expressed my desire to sit behind Bhavna in class, but *maha tharki* Mr Dipendra had indicated his preference and settled himself between her and me. I went to Dipendra and whispered angrily.

"Kamine, she is my target. I've to collect points for ragging."

"Show some maturity," Dipendra retaliated. If someone mentions being mature, it means he thinks he has the license to act immature.

I glared angrily and whispered, "Speak softly and sit here. If you move away now she might catch on, saale tharki."

We planned so thoroughly that we could have been RAW agents and the girls our secret assignments.

Why am I so desperate to sit next to her? I can pay attention to her even from a distance. Besides, I can say anything during the ragging. How'll the seniors figure out what is true? I was shocked at my own immaturity.

Until then, I'd been perfectly sure she was not my next love.

Mr Baloo Pandey, our graphics lab teacher, entered the class. I was excited because he and I shared the same surname. But he acted like Dipendra. He started explaining plans and elevations, paying great attention to the girls. In fact, he turned out to be an even bigger flirt than Dipendra.

Maybe girls need more attention during the labs, I thought to myself in frustration.

Mr Baloo had shown us one half cut diagram and we were made to draw its plan and elevation. All the students were struggling and glancing at each other's desk for help. I tried to reach my target twice, but Dipendra was still sitting between Bhavna and me. I didn't want my horny desire to be recognized by anyone, so I remained seated where I was. I mentally abused him using all the curses I knew.

But Dipendra was already on top of it. Every few minutes, he turned to discuss something with Bhavna. What is an elevation? How do you draw a plan? These were Dipendra's idiotic questions. Anger erupted inside me. Finally, I burst when Dipendra went to Bhavna's desk and started measuring lines against her chart.

Why are you feeling bad, Mr Ajay? They can be friends. It's normal in an engineering college. All the others are also talking and peeking at each other's sheets.

I shifted my anger to Baloo sir. The assignment he'd set was simple. If I asked anyone for anything, it would give the impression that I was dumb.

My false ego had proved the biggest obstacle in breaking the ice with Bhavna. To prove myself a genius, I started explaining stuff to all the others unasked, as if they were dying to receive the much-valued consultancy of Ajay Pandey. I tried twice to reach out to Bhavna. But she looked as busy as a squirrel with its nuts. She didn't look my way even once. Dipendra came to me and said, "Ajay, at least try talking to her once."

"I'm not a despo like you. I'm not a flirt who can talk with no reason," I replied egotistically.

"*Saale phattu.* Coward," Dipendra said, rightly. I didn't counter with an argument.

After an hour of continuous sitting, I had realized that I didn't have courage to talk to her and started focusing on the plan and elevation. I was busy with my sheet and about to complete the assignment when I suddenly heard a sweet, shy voice.

"Do you have any clue on how the plan of this diagram will...Oh, you already finished it."

I stared at the source of the melodic voice. A beautiful girl with killer looks was standing in front of me.

"Do you want any assistance, Bhavna?" I asked, making myself out to be the most intelligent person in the class. Seeing Bhavna, a few more girls started peeping at my worksheet.

My exhibition of smartness went on for a few more minutes and Dipendra was looking aghast and his lips formed the words, "Saala despo."

❖

Bhavna crossed to my aisle when we were about to leave for the day. I decided to say bye to her. I waited desperately as she took tiny steps towards me and the moment she was near enough, I said, "Bye."

"Bye, Ajay," she called back.

We both smiled. I noticed the cute dimples on her cheeks from front for the first time. With that bye, customary drumbeats started rolling in my mind. I reasoned with myself, *Mr Ajay, please hold your horses*. The drumbeats settled down after five minutes of internal celebration.

That was my first interaction with Bhavna.

Freshers' Party Preparations

September 2003
The Freshers' Party

Everyone finds their first college function exciting. We were all pretty cheerful. The seniors would finally stop ragging us. We would be free birds and would be able to explore any part of the institute.

Dipendra and I were among the top ten nominated for the final round of the Mr Fresher contest. Bhavna, Beena and Akansha were also selected from the Electronics Engineering batch to be among the top ten girls for the Miss Fresher title.

Being the first official event, all the freshers were excited about the freshers' party. But the hostellers had their own reasons for happiness. We were happy because we thought that at last the militant ragging would come to an end and we could live peacefully.

Ten boys and ten girls were selected from the freshers' batch and the final five boys and five girls were to be shortlisted based on talent. The final ten would then perform on stage and finally one boy and one girl would be chosen to win the Mr Fresher and Miss Fresher titles.

The competition had multiple rounds like a creative introduction section, question and answer round, behavioural assessments and confidence in speaking in public. All ten finalists assembled in a room. I was excited and tense since it was the first time my newly discovered talent would be evaluated. Bhavna was also there. My mind was making guesses. *Will she dance or sing?* No one in the college was thinking beyond the two categories they seemed to have picked.

"Whether we get shortlisted or not, we'll definitely enjoy this talent hunt round," I giggled to Dipendra.

"Yes, the girls are going to dance in front of us," Dipendra said, expressing his lewd desire.

A jury of ten seniors had arrived. *Wow, what a proud moment!* I was lost in my own daydream which was interrupted by a loud voice. "Ajay Pandey, please come forward."

My name starts with an 'A', so they called me forward first. There is always a first mover advantage in being first, but this theory was going to be proved wrong in my case. I was standing in front of sixty pairs of eyes.

"What are you going to perform for your talent round?" One senior asked

"Mimicry."

"Quite impressive," the senior said. "Go on."

I explained the situation:

This is a fight scene between Sunny Deol and Shahrukh Khan. Sunny threatens Shahrukh, saying that if he continues to stammer, Sunny will kill him with a heavy punch:

"Shahrukh, ye jo tum haqala rahe ho na, kahin dhai kilo ka haath pad gaya to haqlana bandh hojayega. Ye jo dhai kilo ka haath hai, jab padtha hai to aadmi uthata nahi... uth jata hai."

There was complete silence in the room. No one had any reaction and my embarrassment grew. A senior asked, "That was Sunny?"

"Yes," I said but I hoped that was not funny.

"In the second dialogue Shahrukh asks Sunny why he is focusing on his hands. Doesn't he have anything else to focus on?"

"Tum itana haath par focus kyo kar rahe ho, tumhare paas haath hi hai kya...kewal zindagi bhar tumne isi ka istamal kiya hai isiliye dhaai kilo ka ho gaya hai?"

The whole class burst out laughing, and I could see a pair of cheeks dimple. I left the room because the candidates were not allowed to stay there after their audition.

"The first candidate had to perform in front of everyone but the last one only performs in front of the seniors? It's injustice," I shouted in frustration once outside. My desire of seeing the girls dance was destroyed like a house of cards.

Why does my name start with 'A'? It should have been Zandu, I cursed my parents.

But there was no end to my agony. The results came out the same evening and I was disqualified from the competition. Bhavna, Beena and Akansha were selected among the top five female finalists. But then, the worst happened when Dipendra was selected among the top five male finalists. His selection was more painful than my rejection. I was worried now, because he would eat my head and I would not be able to avoid the unbearable display of his talent for dance. I could have forgotten the insult of disqualification if Dipendra would have failed too. But after his selection, I had to bear him till this function lasted. Every time he called me for his dance performance audit, it burnt my heart and soul completely.

❖

I had one more reason to be happy. From that day onwards, I would not have to witness Dipendra's humiliating and sucking dance. I was the only courageous human being who had dared to face his performance after being rejected in the preliminary round.

The seniors had set the last ragging task. All the hostellers had to sit together and cheer for Dipendra. It had been decided that after he had finished his performance, we would have to shout, 'Once more, once more!'

I entered the auditorium which was packed with five hundred students. I sighed, relieved, and thanked God that I had been rejected. I didn't have the courage to face a huge audience. I had been shivering in front of thirty people during my performance in the talent round. Assuming one thousand eyes, ears and five hundred mouths were staring at me even as a dream paralyzed me momentarily.

A few girls came in. Every one of the girls looked different and more beautiful. I was wondering how this transformation had taken place in one day. I received an answer on close observation; no one was wearing those red ribbons. That day I had seen the real engineering girls – no more red ribbons and no more strange clothes. It was not ironical to say that on that day, my Rural Technology college had finally turned to Modern Technology.

Finally, Bhavna entered. Her blackish golden hair was not held back by clips and swung free. Two small golden earrings shone in her ears. She looked like Kajol from the film *Kuch Kuch Hota Hai*. Now, I had two reasons why Kajol was my favourite actress and, ironically, neither had anything to do with her profession. The first, she looked like Bhavna, and the other, she was married to 'Ajay' Devgan. I smiled at my own ridiculous thoughts.

I walked straight up to Bhavna, like a smart chap wanting to flirt with her. She was standing with Akansha. I conveyed my fake wishes to Akansha first.

"All the very best, Akansha. What are you going to perform?"

"Thanks." She passed a fake smile. "Not yet decided," she said.

Now I moved towards my actual target and wished her in an excitement of doing so with a handshake.

"All the best Bhavna, what's up for the talent round?" I said by offering my hand to her. We exchanged a hand shake. Her touch injected some electrons inside me. Obviously some electrons would have to fly after all two Electronic Engineers met.

"Thanks Ajay. I'm not doing much for the talent round. Going to read one poem," Bhavna responded.

I was left with lot of questions. *Why do girls always hide things? They have to perform in front of us after a few hours, anyway. Why are they so secretive about everything? How can someone in the top five say I don't have any talent, I have yet to figure it out. And the other says she is going to read a poem. Thank God I'm not a girl!*

The freshers' party went well and we enjoyed ourselves. As we'd decided, we hooted for Dipendra, shouting, "Once more, once more!"

Even a donkey would have guessed that we were biased, but no one cared.

Akansha danced and I had to agree that she was a good dancer. When it was Bhavna's turn, I was more attentive. Bhavna began reciting a poem attacking the dowry system, and exuded confidence. The way she carried herself didn't indicate that she was facing a crowd of five hundred for the first time.

Bhavna won my heart. She had told me the truth. Gaurav was sitting beside me and yawning, his eyes watering with every yawn.

"What a stupid talent, no dance."

I gave him a dirty look. Perhaps I was the only one watching her attentively.

Finally, the results were announced. Akansha and Tushar turned out to be the winners. I was happy with both the results. Bhavna's defeat kept her in the list of commoners. And had Dipendra won, he would have made my sleeping at night impossible for days to come.

Everyone turned to Akansha to wish her; she was on cloud nine and for good reason. I took this opportunity to talk to Bhavna, taking it upon myself to share her grief. I moved towards Bhavna, remembering the saying that no two girls can be good friends and one can't tolerate defeat at the hands of another girl.

Bhavna was very upset. Normally Bhavna and Akansha stayed together but since Akansha was being congratulated by everyone, Bhavna stood at a distance. I leapt at the opportunity of becoming a shoulder to cry on. I went to her and said, "Congratulations, Bhavna."

"For what?"she asked frustrated.

"Your performance was a good exhibition of oratory skills," I said.

She didn't reply to that, and took her Scooty off its stand.

"I've to leave, something urgent has come up," she said and left. I rarely saw her without a smile. She would have cried if she would have stayed for another minute, and I suspect she cried on her way back.

❖

The same evening, in the hostel, some of my classmates were dancing while a few were playing cards, now that the militant ragging was over. After two months of feeling like we had been living under dictatorship, we were celebrating like a democratic republic now. But the ragging had made a few of us best friends for life.

Everyone was celebrating as if India had won the cricket world cup. Somehow I was not a part of the celebrations. Even I was surprised at my own behaviour.

"The ragging is over, Ajay. We can drink with the seniors," Arvind said to me, shaking his hairy belly. I danced half-heartedly at that. The celebrations went on till one o'clock.

I was about to lose myself in the world of sleep but was distracted by a knock on the door. I turned to Gaurav but he was already fast asleep. I opened the door.

Dipendra, the devil, walked into my room. After the torture of the last two months, 1 a.m. was a normal time for all of us to be awake. He never asked if anyone was sleeping.

After losing the Mr Fresher title, Dipendra was a bit sad. While settling in the chair, he enquired, "How were all the performances?" I know that everyone in the world likes to be praised.

"You were awesome," I said.

"How was my performance, truly?" Dipendra asked, trying to make it sound innocent.

"You were excellent all the way through..," I said, yawning. I was about to finish my statement but he interrupted.

"If I'd given a good answer in the question and answer round, I could have been the winner."

Thank God you lost. If after losing you are praising yourself like this, then God knows what would have happened if you had won!

"How was Akansha's performance? Actually, I was backstage and I didn't get a chance to see it, but I heard that she danced well," Dipendra said. He was asking questions and answering them himself. I was being a good friend and listened to him quietly so that he did not feel let down.

"You know, Bhavna was very sad after the results were announced," I switched to the subject that concerned me.

"That was not fair," Dipendra said.

"What happened?" I blinked. My sleepiness had vanished and I became as attentive as a watchdog.

"Well, Bhavna and Akansha's final scores were the same."

"Then how did Akansha win the title?" I asked, curiously.

"Akansha scored more in the talent round and a senior made the final decision."

"But that is unfair. If the scores were level then Bhavna should have also been given a chance," I said a bit aggressively.

"The seniors were not prepared for a tie breaker."

"But this is unfair."

"Why are you feeling bad, Mr Romeo?" he said with a cunning smile.

"You did not see her. She was really sad. It's the first time I saw such sadness on that beautiful face," I sighed. "Now I understand why she was so disappointed."

"No, she is not aware of this. I just found out an hour ago. The decision was made by three seniors," he revealed. I found this exciting.

"Mr Pandey, you can act quickly," Dipendra said, excited.

Good friends can even understand feelings from faces.

"Now I've to tell her this to win her trust," I shouted. My shout had disturbed the dead man.

"Saale tharki," Gaurav screamed.

❖

I woke up early the next morning at around eight, and left for college by myself. Usually I was accompanied by Dipendra. But I left Dipendra behind on purpose, so that he could not take over my plan of showing Bhavna sympathy. Anyway, he was uncontrollable in front of girls and would surely vomit out everything.

I reached at 9:00 a.m. sharp. Bhavna was already in the class, but Akansha was late.

"Hi. Good morning," I said, sitting down right behind her.

"Hi," she replied.

I stopped myself from telling Bhavna just then because Akansha was not there. *Once she is here I'll tell them everything. Now it's Bhavna's time to feel good,* I thought.

Akansha arrived exactly two minutes later, her smile victorious. I started talking to Bhavna.

"Bhavna, your poem was awesome. Who wrote it?" I asked.

"Don't know. Pooja di gave it to me," Bhavna said half-heartedly.

"Pooja?"

"Yes, Pooja didi is my elder sister," Bhavna was not staying in the hostel. She was living with her family at Allahapur in Allahabad. Her response was a bit bitter. She was not comfortable talking about it. Meanwhile, Akansha came in and settled in the seat adjacent to Bhavna.

"Nice dance, Akansha. Hidden talent."

"Thanks," she blushed and smiled and I took my first shot.

"You guys know? There was a tie between the two of you."

"What? What are you saying? Really?" Akansha exclaimed as I had expected. "Then why was I awarded the title? Why not Bhavna?" Bhavna was now attentive as well. Her face went from pale to pink.

"It's because you scored more in the talent round and the seniors were not prepared for any kind of a tie breaker," I said.

"Who told you this?" Akansha asked.

I mentioned my source. A deathly silence followed. Akansha didn't say anything. It was possible she was still digesting the shocking news. But soon, the silence was broken by a smiling Bhavna.

"Thanks, Ajay," she said.

Now Bhavna's dimples and smile were back. Her thanks resonated in my ears for a long time. She said it once but it echoed as if in an Ekta Kapoor serial. 'Thanks, thanks, thanks. Ajay, Ajay, Ajay.'

And just then, Dipendra entered the classroom.

Pioneer Computers and
my Dreamliner Cycle

The first sessional results were out. As expected, Bhavna scored twenty-four out of thirty, while I scored a six. It was insulting because I was sure next time I would not score any marks. But according to the great Mr tharki Dipendra, we (Bhavna and I) were made for each other as total of our marks were thirty i.e. a hundred percent. He always shares his rubbish gyaan, but this time I retaliated, "If I continue like this, she'll be in the third year and I'll remain in the first year. And together we will complete four years of engineering."

We were the kind of friends who would fight every day, but end up hanging out with each other like real brothers. An invisible thread united us, always. Although we both were tharki, I must say he was my mentor.

I came to know that Bhavna had joined Pioneer Computers for C programming. I too had a reason to join the same institute. But– there is always a 'but' in my story. This time it was money.

I was lost in my agonizing thoughts in my gloomy room.

I have spent my whole life going to coaching classes. Coaching classes in the tenth, the twelfth and after the twelfth I wasted two years at the XL IIT coaching classes in Allahabad. How will my father feel if I ask him for money for coaching classes again? Oh, I cannot ask him for money.

The rational part of mind reasoned,

It's better to spend money on coaching classes rather than wasting money on re-examinations.

Finally, I swallowed and digested a lot of guilt without a single burp and I prepared to join Pioneer Computers. I tried to convince all my dear friends to join the same. Following some rejections, everyone joined C Programming coaching classes.

Dipendra brought a scooter from his home in Rihand. Gaurav and Arvind were the lucky ones, whose asses got the opportunity to kiss the back seat with an explicit condition apply, to share the cost of petrol equally. My inability to share the expenses and the fact that I had a cycle on campus, forced me to ride the cycle. Riding a cycle is always free, so I called my cycle 'Dreamliner'.

Travelling by cycle is quite normal in Allahabad, but it was slightly strange when all the others were travelling by bike and I was the only one travelling by cycle. But who cares if few pennies could be saved, that too for a student like me who only saw money in his dreams. I had a secret desire to be happy. In Allahabad and especially at a college like IERT, a girl and a boy talking to each other raised many eyebrows. But by joining Pioneer Computers, Bhavna had given me a way to talk to her, without a single stranger around. Now, I was free to cross the LOC.

The first day of the coaching class went well. It was the first time I saw her dressed in casuals. She was not wearing the pathan style college uniform but a suit that suited her perfectly. She looked totally different. She had never worn jeans and after seeing her in the new avatar, I felt that suits had been made only for her.

I grabbed the seat next to Bhavna. Half my mind was on Mr Singh, the Sardarji computer teacher, but the other half was on Bhavna. Arvind and Dipendra started teasing me whenever Mr Singh took a break from the lesson. They whispered, "Short-haired friend! Previous crush, Ragini!" I glared at them and they understood that they had crossed the line and held their tongues.

That day after the class, I requested all my hostel pals not to sit beside Bhavna. That seat belonged to me. Thankfully, no one protested. Best friends will die for you if you ask for their help to win a girl, but the irony is that in such a case they will pull you down whenever they get the chance.

Two days had passed and all I had achieved was a 'Hi' on reaching the class and a 'Bye' while leaving. But on the third day, things changed. After sitting patiently near Bhavna, breathing in her scent and gazing at her earrings, I missed a few C programs. After the class, I made a request. "Hey Bhavna, can you please explain the logic behind this program? I missed it."

She started to explain, eyes fixed on my notebook, while the three idiots also peeped in. I winked at them. Dipendra winked and they left, leaving the ground ready for me to make my move.

"Ajay? Ajay, did you understand the logic behind this program?" Bhavna asked.

"Yes, of course," I replied.

Honestly, who cares for C programs when love was about to program? She frowned and we started walking towards the exit. Trying to compliment her, I said, "So Bhavna, you must have scored a good percentage in your tenth and twelfth exams to get in on the management quota, right?" I was aware that she did not appear for the UPSEAT. She had got into this college through the management quota."

"Yes, I did well in the tenth but in the twelfth...."she sighed, "I was not up to the mark."

"What was your score?"

In the tenth, I was the school topper; I scored a 91%. I managed 92% in the twelfth, but stood second," she said, modestly. I went numb but managed to remain calm and standing.

"Ajay,....?" She broke the silence.

"Bad in your twelfth? Unbelievable," I said. She laughed and tried to explain.

"Actually, I studied under the ICSE board. Scoring in the ICSE exams is a bit easier than in the CBSE exams. How much did you score in the tenth and twelfth exams?"

"Hmm... I can't seem to remember exactly but I passed with a first class," I said, careful not to reveal my percentage. She stared at me, doubtfully.

"So, did you join any coaching classes during school?" I asked to keep the conversation rolling.

"My mother taught me until the tenth. I joined coaching classes in the eleventh and twelfth," she explained.

"Mother! Your mother is so intelligent that she taught you until the tenth? What exactly does she do?"

"My mother is a housewife, but she has an MA degree and is pretty strict about our studies."

"An MA degree! During those days," I wooed and she nodded. *Ajay, her mother has studied more than your father*, I thought to myself.

"And what about your father?" I asked, she smiled.

"He has done a number of courses like a B.Sc., an M.Sc., Homeopathy and LL.B."

"Any degree left?" I interrupted. She didn't say anything and my comment felt like a poor joke.

"Sorry," I said.

"My father loves to study," she said. All I heard was the word 'love' coming from her mouth. So what if it was meant for something as boring as studying?

"What exactly does your father do?" she asked.

"My father is an engineer at NTPC, Rihand Nagar Project," I said.

My father was a junior engineer at NTPC, but in order to sound impressive in front of her parent's degrees, I dropped the word junior from his designation. Now, he was promoted to an engineer. *Congratulations Papa, for your sudden promotion.*

I was not comfortable talking to her, so I changed the subject abruptly and asked, "What else do you do Bhavna, apart from studying?" I stressed the last word like I thought it was a sin.

"Hmm, currently, I'm learning how to drive a car."

Oh! It's a massacre! The soldier has been killed in the middle of the field. She owns a car, too. Now it felt unbearable to stand there. Moving towards my cycle, I said, "Okay Bhavna, see you tomorrow. Thanks for your help."

But when you are having the worst moment of your life, it's not swords but words from a beautiful mouth that can kill you.

"Okay, bye, Ajay. But how will you go back?" she asked as her eyes searched for a vehicle among the bikes.

Oh God! Enough embarrassment for one day. While moving towards my Dreamliner, I gathered all my courage and determination and said, "I have a cycle. Good night, Bhavna. Bye."

I said a hurried 'bye' so that there was no scope for further embarrassment. I started cursing myself on the way to the hostel.

"You fool! Her mother and father are so educated. She has a car and rides a Scooty every day. And you, Mr Romeo? Look at yourself! You have a Boeing 767 dreamliner to commute!" I scolded myself. "Mr Lover Boy, please focus on your studies."

I began to direct my anger towards God. "What the hell is this, God? Why this injustice? Why, why, why?"

There are thousands of coaching institutes in Allahabad. As my cycle crept towards the hostel, I saw a big hoarding in front of a coaching institute.

Don't think of what you'll receive. Think of what you'll leave for others.

"I want to leave this Dreamliner cycle behind!" I yelled, frustrated.

The Most Romantic Hour
of My Life

A few more days passed, and my bond with Bhavna grew stronger. But the more I learned about Bhavna's background, the more I was tempted to withdraw from the friendship. Every alternate day, after my class ended, I used to cycle to the hostel while three of my friends zoomed past me on the scooter, taunting me with shouts of, "Bye Pandey." Bhavna, too, would zoom past me saying, "Bye, Ajay".

I would follow her with my eyes as long as I could see her. The situation was ironic. I felt like a slow tortoise crawling by as my friends zoomed past like rabbits, yelling goodbyes.

This tragic tale continued, when finally, something unexpected happened on the tenth day of class. I was cycling towards the hostel as usual with my friends zooming past me, each shouting a humiliating, 'Bye Pandey.' I was enraged and showed them the middle finger as I continued on my way. When I didn't hear Bhavna's mellow goodbye for another 200 meters, I decided to turn around and look for her.

I found her white Scooty standing in its usual place outside the Pioneer Coaching Centre but its pretty owner was missing. I looked around and saw the familiar boyish crop of hair emerge from a nearby PCO. Bhavna looked worried.

"What's up, Bhavna?" I asked.

"I was calling my father. My Scooty has broken down," Bhavna said.

I looked at my Dreamliner and hated it all over again. If only I had a bike, I would have been able to drop her home.

"So is your father coming to pick you up?" I asked.

"No Ajay, Papa will not be coming. He is busy at the bank. He'll be free around nine and I can't wait till then. I'll have to manage on my own," she replied, worried.

Her father worked as a manager in a nationalized bank.

"There is an auto mechanic shop near Jagat Taran College, about 400 meters away," I replied hopefully, trying to conceal my inner joy.

She thought for a second and said, "Okay, let's go there."

Her Scooty was too heavy for her to wheel so I asked her courteously, "Do you want to exchange vehicles?"

"No, I'm fine."

"Have you ever wheeled a bicycle? Today could be your lucky day!"

She smiled, despite the obvious effort it took her to pull her broken down Scooty along and said, "No, thanks, Ajay. I'll manage."

"Okay, as you wish, but you are missing a great opportunity to pull the Pandeyji chariot." She laughed and the sight of her dimples blew me away.

"Thanks for coming," she said shyly. "It would have been difficult, otherwise."

I tried to make her exchange vehicles, again. "Please try pulling my chariot. It's better than a king's vehicle, believe me. It is very special," I said, flirtatiously.

"Okay, oh King. The honour is mine," she chuckled as we exchanged vehicles. My cycle was being wheeled by such a beautiful maiden for the first time.

"Sorry Ajay, for involving you in all this. It is only 400 meters, right?" she questioned.

"Totally fine, Bhavna."

Why just 400 metres? I would be happy to walk 400 kilometres with you.

My wrist watch said it was 7:15 p.m. and everything suddenly seemed more beautiful. The fast approaching darkness also helped the situation. For the first time, the September breeze felt comforting. The moon appeared to swell in size. And to top it all, a beautiful and smart girl was walking with me. I was almost engulfed in the happiness of the moment.

"Can I ask you something, Ajay?" she questioned and I nodded in acquiescence.

"Who is Ragini? I'm sorry if it is intrusive, but I heard your friends tease you about her."

I fell silent. *Should I tell her the truth about my relationship with Ragini? That there is nothing between us and we are only good friends?* I pondered and decided to use her curiosity to my advantage

"Actually Ragini used to be my girlfriend," I said, looking embarrassed.

"She used to be? Does that mean...?" she asked, eagerly.

"Yes, actually she is pursuing an engineering degree from Bhopal and I'm here, in Allahabad. So there is very little interaction between us, which is why I'm thinking about ending things with her," I said quietly.

Meanwhile, we'd reached our destination – the Scooty repair shop. The mechanic checked her Scooty by trying to kick start it after which he said, "Pin change *karna padega. Carburettor ko bhi saaf karna hoga, ek ghanta lagega.*" He had to change the pin and clean the carburettor. It would take an hour.

If the mechanic had been a girl I would have kissed him for saying it would take an hour.

"Bhaiya, please. Fix it fast," Bhavna requested.

"Hundred rupees," the mechanic said, quoting his price.

"Please start your work," she instructed.

I was lost in my own daydreams while she was talking to him. *What a day. One whole hour, just Bhavna and I together. Please use it well, bro.*

"Relax, Bhavna. Bhaiya take your time but do it well," I told the mechanic. "Bhavna, don't you worry. I'm here," I whispered. "If you rush, he might not fix it properly, understand?"

She nodded. We stood on the side of the road and started talking to each other.

"How many siblings do you have, Ajay?" Bhavna asked.

"There are three of us. I'm the middle child. My elder sister is pursuing a degree in fashion design and my younger brother is in class 10."

"Why are you thinking of breaking up with Ragini? Is it only because there is less interaction?" she asked curiously about Ragini. Her hidden jealously excited me.

"There is one more reason, I must admit. She belongs to a rich family and our lifestyles are not compatible," I said intentionally to see her reaction. By putting Ragini in the middle, I was cooking my chicken around Bhavna.

She thought for a while and asked, "Who proposed to whom first?"

"Ragini proposed to me," I lied, like I was the famous Shahrukh Khan and Ragini was dying to be with me.

"Look, Ajay, Ragini seriously loves you. Money doesn't matter to her," she said. "You should not be under such an illusion." I felt happy.

"Everyone in her family is well qualified. In fact, her mother was a teacher at my school," I said, planting another fact intentionally and waiting for her reaction.

"Come on, Ajay. All these things sound silly."

"How can you say this so firmly? Have you...have you ever been in such a relationship?" I asked with a heavy heart, hoping an answer in negative. My heart was running a marathon. I was about to get a cardiac arrest but she saved me.

"No, Ajay. I never had an affair or any of that stuff. Pooja di has one with a guy. And knowing what they went through, I can say your reasons seem silly compared to what real lovers go through," she replied.

"But for real lovers," I sighed and she seemed to fall into deep thought. It was dangerous to make a beautiful mind work. I fired my other question.

"What does Pooja di's boyfriend do?" I asked with intent, trying to compare myself with him.

"Calling him 'would-be-jiju' is better," she said. "The word boyfriend doesn't sound serious."

So I'm your would be husband, I thought.

"Okay, what is your *would be jiju* doing?' I grinned ironically and thought, such intense love, saying would be *Jiju*.

"He is studying with Pooja di."

"So Bhavna, can I ask you a personal question?"

"Of course."

"Why did you cry after the results of the freshers' party competition were announced?"

"Oh, you noticed that? I was with Beena the whole time and even she didn't notice."

"A true friend sees the first tear, catches the second and stops the third," I said intentionally, hoping these lines were not too much.

"Yes, a good friend. A true friend, actually," she murmured, then smiled and sighed.

"You felt bad because you had lost?" I poked again.

"I don't know, but it felt good when you told us about the tie between me and Akansha."

"What is your date of birth, Ajay?" she asked, changing the topic. Maybe she was still not comfortable discussing that episode.

"Eighth of July," I answered.

"Wow, you are a Cancerian and you were born on the eighth, too!"

Girls are really weird. My birth date never excites me, or my family.

"What is exciting about being a Cancerian?" I shrugged. "Are you also a Cancerian, or what?"

"No, I'm a Scorpion but my birth date is the same as yours. The eighth of November," she said, happy.

Cancerian and Scorpion sounded like Troy and Spartan to me. I was confused. Is being born on the same date a reason for happiness?

"What time is it, Ajay?" she asked, concerned.

"A quarter past eight."

Bhavna worriedly asked the mechanic, "Bhaiya, *kitna time aur lagega?* How long will it take?" The word 'bhaiya' echoed in my mind. It seemed so disgusting.

Thank god I'm not a mechanic, I thought.

"Almost done. Two minutes more, madam," the mechanic answered.

"Bhavna, isn't your father worried? I mean, he didn't send someone to help you," I asked, concerned.

"Actually, my papa wants his kids to be independent," she sighed. "He always says I am his son."

"Nice thought. Quite a logical person," I said, praising her father intentionally. "So don't you have any brothers?"

"No Ajay, I don't have any brothers. That's why my father wants to make us strong and confident, so that we can handle small problems like this independently. It is only us two sisters," she said in a low voice and stared sadly.

She went silent, and I, retrospective. Did she miss having a brother? The way she stared at me the moment I thought this, I felt she would call me 'bhaiya'.

No, Bhavna I'm not your brother. Run Ajay! Run! Before she calls you 'bhaiya'. And you did make a mistake by mentioning Ragini, I said to myself.

I was about to say, 'Sorry, Bhavna. I'm getting late for dinner. The mess serves dinner only till 9.00 p.m.' when I was interrupted.

"It's done," the mechanic said, suddenly.

"Good timing," I murmured.

"Hundred rupees," the mechanic reminded us.

"Take eighty, bro. Student-discount," I negotiated.

Allahabad is the only place where a majority asks for discounts as there are students everywhere. They can seek a discount at any shop. Even the tea maker charges one rupee less from students. Finally, the mechanic agreed to take eighty rupees. Bhavna smiled at my bargaining skills.

"Bye, Bhavna," I said getting on my cycle.

"Thank you, good friend and good night." When she said the word 'good', it felt like I was receiving a gallantry award.

I was on cloud nine on my way to the hostel. My head was spinning. I felt so much in love. I drove my cycle at a slow speed; now this turtle was happier crawling. I kissed the handlebars of my cycle and said, "Sorry, dear. I had a chance to spend one valuable hour with Bhavna because of you. Otherwise, I would have been on my way back like the others."

I swayed on my cycle and began singing:

'Ek ladki ko dekha to aisa laga, jaise khilta gulab, jaise shayar ka khwab, jaise ujali kiran, jaise bun mein hiran, jaise chandni raat, jaise narmi ki baat, jaise mandir main ho ek jalta diya...'

So lost was I in my dreams that I ended up reaching the hostel at around 9:30 p.m.

The mess was closed.

"Please see if there is something to eat," I pleaded with the mess staff.

"Nothing, bhaiya. Everything is finished," the mess worker answered.

But my repeated requests softened him.

"Only some daal is left. You want to eat it? No rice, no chapatti."

"Please give it to me."

I had that daal with internal customary drum beats. I had it like I was having the world's most special cuisine. Only a person in love can enjoy such a dish.

It's easy to make friends, but difficult to keep them

Talking about my fake relationship with Ragini had worked in my favour. Bhavna was now more comfortable talking to me. She added me to her safe zone. Girls always like the saga of friendship, but boys use this friendship to climb the ladder of love.

I was happier, more cheerful and smiled a lot more than before, because I had the chance to talk to Bhavna twice every alternate day. Our friendship had moved beyond the fake 'hellos' and 'byes'.

I started liking her more. I don't know whether it was a crush or love, but for sure, I liked her: the way she carried herself, her smile, her earrings, her hairstyle and her ever-helping attitude. In short, she was a girl who was a saint for everyone.

It was the beginning of November. I went to Dipendra's room.

"Dipendra, Bhavna's birthday is on the 8th of November," I said, concerned as if a national calamity was about to occur. "What should I gift her? Can you suggest something nice and cheap for Bhavna's birthday?" I asked. I could only discuss 'cheap' things with my hostel pals.

"Are you mad? Wasting money on girls is futile," Dipendra retorted.

"She is not just any girl," I said. "She is my prospective wife." I used the word 'wife' very carefully, because for Dipendra, love and sex were the same thing.

"Your parents have sent you here to study and you guys waste your money and time on these girls," Dipendra spouted some old Hindi movie dialogue.

"Mr Dipendra, will you please focus on the gift," I shouted, irritably. When it comes to girls, boys will always stretch the matter until you shout at them.

"What is your budget?" he asked. That was the million dollar question for a guy like me.

"Thirty or fifty rupees."

He gave me a worried frown, "Okay, eighty maximum." I increased my limit from thirty to eighty with great difficulty.

"Buy a Hallmark or Archies card and give it to her with a bouquet," he suggested.

"A card and a bouquet?" I yelled. "A card is so useless and flowers die after two days."

"Mr Millionaire, nothing will fit in this budget. Moreover, girls are emotional; they like cards, and the entire card industry runs because of them." He made another suggestion. "You can do one thing. You can contribute and we can gift something together."

"No contributions," I sensed my possessiveness for her.

"Look Mr Romeo, give her a card with chocolate. You can even get them for less than fifty rupees," he said with a cunning smile, as if he'd solved a brainstorming electronic puzzle.

❖

I went to University Road near Katra. It was a street famous for textbooks and other crazy stuff students would be interested in.

I went into a card shop where I found thousands of cards for all occasions – apologies, proposals, farewells, anniversaries, thank yous, New Year, Mother's Day, Father's, and a lot more. I was shocked. Who buys all these? But when I turned my head to look, I found many girls in the shop. I recalled Dipendra's words; "The entire industry runs because of these girls."

I browsed five birthday cards but every card had a red heart on it. I was a bit surprised; what was a heart doing on a birthday card? Finally, I managed to find one birthday card without any hearts on it. Now, that 'heartless' card was going to communicate what I had in my heart.

After selecting a card, I faced another dilemma. What would I write on it? This began to bother me even more. Eureka! I looked through a few more friendship cards and found a few lovely lines. I looked around, and when I was sure no one was watching me, I took out a paper and pen from my bag and noted the lines. My old habit of cheating in exams was finally paying off.

I bought a sparkle pen and a chocolate too. I had never purchased such an expensive chocolate myself, but I felt it was my destiny that my first expensive chocolate would be a gift for someone else.

Back in the boys' hostel, I started to practice writing with the thick sparkle pen on rough sheets. But after seeing my own writing I realized that if I was unable to decipher my Chinese or Japanese, how would Bhavna? I had committed a sin. I went to Dipendra and requested him to help me.

"Can you write for me? My writing is a bit poor and this sparkle pen is making it worse."

He wrote what I'd copied in the shop. In my room, I lay on my bed, thinking. *I should write something on my own. After all, I genuinely have feelings for her.*

After spending millions of seconds and utilizing the strength of all the nerves of my nervous system, I could just write one line. *It's easy to make friends, but difficult to keep them.*

❖

8 November 2003
Bhavna's birthday

A lot of her friends were demanding a birthday treat, so she had to give a small party in the college canteen. She also received a few gifts. I wished her a happy birthday in college and asked whether she would be coming for the coaching class that day. She confirmed that she would, so I decided to give her my card after the class, so that the other girls wouldn't notice it. Girls have a habit of investigating the gifts given by guys.

After the Pioneer Class, future lovebirds Bhavna and I began a conversation when everyone had left.

"Where is my birthday gift?" Bhavna asked.

"How are you so sure that I bought something for you?"

"How can my best friend not give me a gift today," she said, softly. It was really touching. I was mesmerized with these amiable words and felt like kissing her cheeks, but I controlled my one-sided desire.

I opened my bag and gave her my most precious chocolate. "Oh! Nice chocolate, but I think you have something else, too," she said peeping inside my bag.

She was so curious that she gave the chocolate back to me and flipped the card open. "Wow! What a nice card," she exclaimed, blissfully. *What's so special about this?* I wondered.

She read the message and asked in a low voice, "Who has written this?" Her words hit me.

"I...I...I have written it," I said, but the 'I' sounded hollow.

"This is not your writing; its Dipendra's," she said, her words hitting me, again. My heart began beating uncontrollably. Thank god, I wasn't a heart patient else I would have taken off.

"Actually, Dipendra wrote it, but the words are mine," I said, swallowing my own saliva, like mango pulp.

"Ajay, you are a good friend of mine. The card hardly matters to me. Will you please tell the truth?"she said, assertively.

"I wrote this line," I said pointing to the line, "and the rest was written by Dipendra." I hid the fact that I'd copied from another card.

Then we shared the chocolate. It's always good to gift someone chocolates, because you end up getting a bit of it. And if someone is a Brahmin like me, then they get the most.

"Bhavna, how did you guess that it wasn't my writing?" I asked puzzled. She laughed madly; sometimes her laughter humiliates me.

"Mr Dipendra asked me after the class how I liked your card and after opening the card I found two different styles of handwriting. So I guessed the rest." She laughed again. *All beautiful girls are not dumb*, I thought to myself.

"That was the biggest mistake I made. He can't digest anything." I said.

Kamine Dipendra. I'll kill you!

"Ajay, I have to go now, since I've to go for dinner at Elchico in Civil Lines with my family," she said while wheeling her Scooty away from the parking lot.

Elchico! Expensive restaurant!

I felt a bit low since I had been caught red handed. To cheer me up, she said, "One compliment for Ragini. She has a nice, simple hearted person."

That nice, simple person belongs to you, not Ragini, I wanted to say.

"Okay. Wish you a very happy birthday again," I said while shaking her hand.

Then I bid her goodnight. She started her Scooty and said, "Good night Ajay. By the way, there was only one line in card that I liked the most – 'it's easy to make friends, but difficult to keep them'."

She left but her last words made my day. I even pardoned that devil Dipendra. I felt annoyed with myself. *Why did I create a fake love triangle with Ragini? My progress was smooth. Unnecessarily dragging Ragini into it had made it a triangle. How will Bhavna react when she finds out the truth?*

How do I propose?

By now I was quite sure that Bhavna wasn't just a crush. I was definitely in love with her. But, I felt trapped in a one-sided affair, again. Now, I was eager to break my age old hitch of one-sided affairs. A one-sided affair is like constructing a mansion over someone else's land. This time it would be my land.

It was our last day at Pioneer Computers. On my way, I wondered how to propose to her.

Today is the last day. And from tomorrow, it's possible that I'll not get an opportunity to talk to her. Shall I propose to her directly or express my feelings indirectly? If she accepts, then everything will be just perfect. But, in case she does not, maybe I'll lose my friendship with her.

The spiral of thoughts continued.

Shall I ask for her phone number? But, again, how will she call me? I don't even have a cell phone. What a beggar I am. But Dipendra has a cell phone. Will she be alright with calling me on Dipendra's cell? Why is it so important to propose to anyone? Can't we be just friends?

All these crazy thoughts raged like a storm inside my mind. Practising to propose your love to a girl is like rehearsing to win a gold medal at the Olympics.

After the class, in the parking lot, I walked up to her. "How are you feeling about the coaching classes ending today, Bhavna?"

"Not good and am a bit scared," her tone hid her nervousness.

"Scared? Why?"

"I still don't have confidence in my programming skills," she replied quietly.

I felt bad. I thought she would feel sad that we wouldn't have the chance to chat like this once the coaching classes ended. But her thoughts seemed unrelated.

"I'm pretty confident about my programming skills, so you can discuss it with me, anytime, over the phone," I said, instead of asking for her number directly.

She giggled and said, "Sure, anytime." It sounded like my confidence in programming was a joke to her.

BSNL was the market leader in those days and the mobile market had not grown much. I was aware that Bhavna did not have a cell phone as well.

She smiled, "You can have my landline number. But I'm sorry, Ajay, you can't call."

"What is the use of having a weapon if you can't fire it?" I said, sarcastically.

"Look Ajay, my parents have a problem if a guy calls. Especially mummy." She sighed.

"But why? You're studying with boys in a co-educational institution and you have to interact with them during labs and projects," I argued, hiding my desperation.

She hesitated a bit and said, "If a boy calls, it means he is a friend and tomorrow that friend could be a boyfriend and then..." she shrugged. I was surprised at how causally she had said this, when it was what I was actually hoping would happen.

"Okay, Bhavna, I understand. If someone called my sister at home, my parents would also feel the same way," I said, backing her up so that she would not feel bad.

We would have preparation leave from college in two days. This would be followed by exams and then a ten-day semester break. This meant that I would meet my one-sided love after two months and there would be no possibility of chatting on the phone, either. My internal calculations increased my grief.

"Ajay, you look a bit sad today. What happened?" she asked.

"It's because of Ragini. Now it's not possible to continue a relationship with her. She is going around with other guys in Bhopal," I said, hiding the real reason for my sadness.

"Ajay, if she is happy with someone else, let her be. Exams are coming up. I don't want my friend to be distracted because of someone who doesn't even care for him," she said.

"Bhavna, suppose I have doubts, and I want to discuss them during our preparation leave, is there any way that I can reach you?"

She thought and said something that felt like a mockery of me. "Do you have a cell phone?"

A person for whom eighty rupees worth of gifts for his love seemed like a million dollar deal, affording a cell phone was impossible. "Ma'am, if I had that, I would have shared my number a long time back," I sighed. "But Dipendra has a cell phone and he spends most of his time with me."

She thought for a while, "No, Ajay. I can't call Dipendra. It won't look good if I call Dipendra's number and ask for you."

"No, just call on his number. He won't pick up. Only I'll answer your call."

She looked suspiciously at me. Immediately, I realized the slip of tongue and corrected the mistake, "See, have you ever called Dipendra? No, then I'll tell him you are calling me to discuss something related to studies and to transfer that call to me."

She didn't say anything and I felt miserable again. Bhavna noticed this. She must have thought that I was sad because of Ragini.

To cheer me up she said, "Let's celebrate today as if it's a farewell party for the coaching class."

"Celebrate?" I said, dismally. *Is she crazy or what? What do we have to celebrate here?*

"Do you like paani poori?"she asked cheerfully. *I don't like paani poori much.*

"I love paani poori. It's my favourite," I said, to indulge her. *Perhaps I can replace paani poori with her name.*

"Chhappan Bhog has the best paani poori. It's near Civil Court in Kacheri," she suggested.

"Let's move, then."

You can find two kinds of shops in any corner of Allahabad; tea shops and paani poori stalls. But I don't know what was so special about Chhappan Bhog. We started heading towards Kacheri Road. I was crawling along on my cycle and she was driving her Scooty beside me.

What an idiot she is? She should have offered me a lift since I can't offer her one on my cycle.

I tried to console myself. *Please understand, Ajay. Family values. A girl roaming around with a guy could become IERT gossip and roaming in Allahabad at 7:30 p.m. is taboo.*

Just before we reached Chhappan Bhog, Bhavna encountered another girl on Scooty, who stopped in front of her and said, "Hi, Bhavna."

Is this Pooja di? I started getting goosebumps but my body returned to normalcy after listening to their conversation.

"Hi, Priya! Long time," Bhavna replied.

Now, I understood why Bhavna had not offered me a lift. Priya stared at me; we exchanged a hello with fake smiles.

"My friend from engineering. I was going to Chhappan Bhog and just met him on the way," Bhavna explained, before her friend could fire any questions at her. Priya whispered something in Bhavna's ear. Both of them chuckled, and then Priya left. Girls always laugh at their own poor jokes.

At Chhappan Bhog, Bhavna ordered two plates of paani poori. She seemed elated. "Bhaiya, chutney also," she said to the man serving us the paani poori. How did this paani poori stuff excite her so much?

"What was Priya whispering?" I asked, lost in my own agony.

She put the paani poori in her mouth, making her face looked completely round. She didn't say anything and waved her hand to signal that she would explain it later. That dish was her favourite and no one should disturb her. But my needle got stuck on Priya's fake smile. When the paani poori was gobbled up, I asked,

"So what did Priya say? Is she a good friend of yours?"

Instead of replying to my question, she smiled and asked, "How was the paani poori?"

I hadn't even noticed its taste, but I was happy that she had enjoyed it. To delight her I said, "The paani poori was awesome." I sighed. "What did Priya say?" I reiterated the question like a parrot.

"She was my classmate at St Mary's Convent and she whispered, 'Boyfriend?' And I replied, 'No, just friend'."

It killed me. The whole world could guess my actions but nothing seemed to be moving in my favour. I was about to say goodbye to Bhavna.

Then, she said, "Ajay, whenever you feel there is a genuine reason to talk, just give two short missed calls with a gap of five seconds from Dipendra's cell phone and I'll call you back on his number."

"Why two?" I asked, excited. "Why not one?"

"After one missed call, it is Pooja didi who calls jiju," she laughed.

"Would be Jiju?"

"Yes," she nodded.

That could have been the reason her mother resented boys. Mr Would be Jiju was enjoying his first mover advantage.

"But remember, Ajay, only you should answer my call, not Dipendra, and..." She paused for a second and I broke in to say, "But, what...?"

"There should be a genuine reason for the call," she said seriously. After boosting my luck, she had suddenly pressed the button of despair.

I started pedalling my cycle towards the IERT hostel as Bhavna headed towards Allahpur. While parting she shouted, "All the very best for exams!"

"Same to you and remember, never surrender," I said.

"Never surrender, what?" she asked.

"Never surrender means, never give up. One of my favourite lines." I don't know why I said so, but I had learnt it while I was reading about World War II. Never surrender in a war. Maybe I had begun to treat love as a kind of war as well.

"Impressive line." She gave an expression of appreciation, "Much required for exam preparations." A studious girl always takes thing accordingly.

I bid her bye for the day and while moving she said, "Ajay, you deserve a better girl than Ragini." She smiled like a model in a Close-up ad. Her final words made my day.

I said to myself, *Yes, the better one is you.*

❖

Dipendra's phone was like oxygen for me. The college was closed for exam preparation. Now that I could chat with Bhavna, it wasn't something I was concerned about because I had to focus on my first engineering exams. These exams were scary. We had not yet covered the syllabus and we could be asked questions from anywhere. Guessing exam questions was like searching for pearls in the ocean.

I was under twice the amount of pressure to perform. First, I had to do well to pull my family out of its money crunch; and second, I had to win the heart of my love who had stood first in the tenth and second in the twelfth. Obviously, I found the second reason more motivating.

During exams, after analyzing my answer sheet and looking at my Chinese hand writing, the idea of competing with Bhavna was crushed. Whenever I finished my paper before the allotted time, I never scrutinized it because the sight of my handwriting worried me. I realized a bitter truth – there was no way I was going to score more than Bhavna in the engineering exams.

She used to call me the evening before the exam and inquire about my preparation. She would wish me luck. But, whenever she called me, I was always ready with some doubts, so that the conversation lengthened for some more minutes. She was really concerned and helpful. She always took out sufficient time to explain. On the other hand, I never bothered to listen. I was only happy with the fact that she was talking to me.

Once I said, "Bhavna, you have been explaining the chapter for the last fifteen minutes. Your phone bill will skyrocket."

"Not to worry. It's sponsored by UCO Bank," she said and laughed.

The way she cared for me and called me before every exam was itself a proof that she liked me. But, she was always concerned, sensitive and emotional about everyone. I told you she was a saint for everyone.

On the last day of the exam, I gave Bhavna my Rihand Nagar landline number because we had ten days holidays. All my friends were excited to go home, and I was the only jerk who was feeling low.

At home in Rihand Nagar, I sat in front of my heavy, old BSNL phone that rang so loudly that even the neighbours knew someone was calling Pandeyji's house. But I didn't get any calls from her.

❖

Once the second semester started, Bhavna and I turned into 'hi' and 'bye' kind of friends. Again. We exchanged a 'hi' in morning while I kept staring at her like a peacock that was waiting for rain and received a 'bye' at the end of the day.

She was always with Beena. Beena and Bhavna, both their names started with 'B' and that seemed to have drawn them closer still. They were in the same batch for every lab and every assignment. She didn't talk to me much because interactions between girls and boys turned into college gossip. Some gossip had already spread about the two of us, and that increased the distance between us.

January 2004

I was in the hostel and I began to feel sad, missing the lovely days we had spent together at Pioneer Computers. I remembered all our past memories and cursed myself for not having the money to buy a phone.

Then a shrewd idea stuck me. The NTPC had a nice medical reimbursement policy. All expenses are covered if medicines and treatment are prescribed by registered doctors and if you have proof. I went to the small clinic outside the campus which had a small sign saying Indian Medical Association with a cross and a snake on it. I never understood why the Indian Medical Association had chosen such a sign. It was possible that they had treated people poisoned by snakes in the past.

I explained the symptoms seriously. My mother was asthmatic and I knew the cost of an inhaler. Asthma inhalers are hand-held portable devices that deliver medication to lungs. A flop mimicry actor inside me gave his best performance.

I also told him that I would be travelling for the next few months and asked him to to prescribe three inhalers. The doctor recommended three inhalers along with five strips of tablets and said, "You can discontinue these medicines after five days, if you have recovered by then."

"Consultancy fees, sir?" I asked.

"Hundred rupees."

"Student discount, sir?" I pleaded.

He softened and charged me fifty rupees. I went straight to a medical shop and requested the shopkeeper to just make a bill.

"For how many days?" the shopkeeper asked.

"I only want a bill for fifteen days."

"Our cut is ten percent, but for a student like you, we'll take five percent."

"What is the final bill?"

"One thousand six hundred and fifty rupees."

"Great!" I said with a winning smile. It was definitely rare for someone to feel happy on seeing such a large medical bill.

I called Papa and explained that I wasn't well and would courier the prescription with the bill to him. I felt bad but imagining talking to Bhavna on the phone was enough to absolve me from self-guilt. The next morning, Papa transferred three thousand rupees into my SBI account. Parents always add a little extra in case of an emergency. I'd already saved about a thousand rupees. Finally, I was all set to enter the telecom world.

❖

It was time for the annual sports events of our institution. Bhavna and Beena participated in a badminton tournament. I went to her during the practice session. "My father has gifted me this Nokia 3315 cell phone." I lied, showing her a bulky silver bricklike device. She pressed a button on my cell phone and found only two numbers were saved. One was hers and the other was my home. She gave a doubtful look. We exchanged numbers and said bye. I returned to the hostel with high hopes.

Five days had passed. In spite of making a huge investment on the silver cell phone, she hadn't called even once. My fate remained unchanged. My hopes were dashed. I felt gloomy and felt like Bhavna was slipping away from me. I was infected by the Devdas syndrome, whose lover Paro was running away from him and there was no scope for another Chandra Mukhi as well. All my happiness vanished. I decided that I couldn't carry the burden of this one-sided love any more. I had to tell her, whether she accepted it or not.

I conspired and since Valentine's day was approaching, I decided to propose to her before that. I assigned a date to myself.

It was the first week of February. I went to Bhavna in the parking lot.

Bhavna and I were alone, facing each other. Since we hardly spoke now, I had missed her a lot. I felt like hugging her, but my thoughts were interrupted by her sweet voice.

"What happened, Ajay? You are not the same guy I knew."

"I'm not well, Bhavna. I'm suffering from viral fever," I lied, again.

"No, Ajay. Don't try to hide it. I've noticed over the last few days, you aren't being the jolly and cheerful person you used to be," she said.

I felt a bit happy. At least she had been paying attention to me. Then, I executed my plan, "I lied to you, Bhavna. Actually I've planned to leave IERT forever."

"Forever! Why? What happened?" she asked.

"I'm getting admission into DAVV Indore. I'll be joining the second semester directly through some links my father has. It's a better college with regards to placements than IERT."

I lied to Bhavna to observe her reaction; if she loved me, she would definitely feel bad about my decision. I'd chosen DAVV Indore, because one of my friends was studying there and I knew even the smallest detail about it.

I was observing her carefully to see whether she was sad about the news of my sudden departure. But the girl who was an angel for everyone, sometimes behaved like a demon to me. "Ajay, parents are always concerned about their children. If they are making you do something, then you should listen to them."

I held my head and thought, *Why had I fallen for such a good girl?*

❖

A few more days went by. I was filled with confusion about whether she loved me or not. It felt like there was a group discussion inside my head all the time. A part of my brain said that she loved me like a friend and would accept my love once I told her about it. Another part countered that she had never loved me, and that she was just an emotional girl who cared about everyone. My mind was being destroyed by the war between these positive and negative thoughts. My health, my studies and my head were beginning to get affected. I always lay on my bed and kept an eye on my heavy, silver Nokia handset, waiting for it to ring. It was almost like a virgin girl hoping to get pregnant.

I decided to put an end to all of it. It was better to die with clarity, rather than live with fake hopes on a ventilator.

On 7th February in the common room of the boys' hostel, I was flipping through the newspaper and came across some interesting news. An international festival called Valentine's Week was about to start. The newspaper had printed an entire love calendar. It was to begin with Rose Day, followed by Proposed Day, Chocolate Day, Teddy Day, Promise Day, Kiss Day, Hug Day and finally D-Day or Valentine's Day. It had been perfectly scheduled from the seventh to the fourteenth of February.

So in accordance with the paper, I would have to propose to her the next day or the 8th of February. But another newspaper revealed some new information. Its post-Valentine's love calendar stated that 15 February was Slap Day, 16 February was Kiss Day, 17 February was Perfume Day, 18 February was Flirting Day, 19 February was Confession Day, 20 February was Missing Each Other Day and 21 February was Breakup Day.

I failed to understand the reason for this order, but the last day was an eye opener: Breakup Day? Even marketing executives felt that love lasted only two weeks. I dumped those newspapers and decided to follow my own destiny.

A new idea popped into my cunning mind. I would write a letter to Bhavna with all my feelings for her. I had written two pages in my Chinese hand-writing, but another positive part of my mind came up with another idea: *You care for her, she should realize that. Giving her love letters could also create confusion about whether they were written by you or not?*

I dropped this plan as well and shouted to God, "How do I propose?"

Love you, Bhavna

13 February 2004
The day before Valentine's Day

I decided to propose to Bhavna on 13 February. It was a deliberate choice to propose to her before D-Day, knowing that girls need some time to think about things. There was a huge chance that she would fall into the trap of wanting to celebrate Valentine's Day which could lead her to accept my proposal. It was madness to expect such a thing from a girl like her, but love is not only blind, it's dumb too.

I didn't go to college on the thirteenth. I was caught up in my own crazy preparations. I collected some of Bhavna's things like her freshers' party performance photographs, some of her notes, a photocopy that she had given to me and even rough sheets that she had used to explain C programming to me.

At around six in the evening, when I was just going to execute my plan, my phone vibrated; someone was calling me from a landline.

"Hi, Ajay. Bhavna here." Her call was like a drizzle in Jaisalmer.

"Hi," I replied.

"Ajay, tomorrow is my badminton match and Gaurav is my partner in the mixed doubles. Can you give him a message and tell him to reach college soon? Tell him to be at the auditorium for practice at around 4 p.m. tomorrow," she said quickly, trying to finish the call within sixty seconds.

"Ok sure, where are you calling from?"

"A PCO booth near Prayaag railway station."

I asked for the exact location. Prayaag Station was close to IERT and I knew every place around it.

"Bhavna, please be there. I'm coming to meet you. It's urgent."

"Ajay, I'm getting late. Can we talk tomorrow?"

"Bhavna, it's my last day at IERT. Tomorrow I'm leaving for DAVV Indore forever, remember?"

"Oh, yeah! Okay, I'm waiting. Come soon."

"Listen Bhavna, I want to meet you alone." I said hastily but still could not match up with the telecom frequency; it echoed with dirty *tooon tooon* sound. She had hung up the phone.

I took all her stuff and started pedalling my cycle to take the bravest step of my life. On my way, I started collecting my thoughts and practicing what I had to say. I kept talking to myself. "Never surrender Ajay, you can." I reached the PCO after a ten-minute ride.

My jaw dropped when I saw Beena standing with Bhavna. I didn't even say 'hi' to either of them and just stared at Beena. She was really perceptive. After seeing my dismay, she bid goodbye to Bhavna and left. Maybe my pale face conveyed my feelings to her.

Now Bhavna and I were alone.

"What happened, Ajay? Why did you want to see me all of a sudden?"

"Bhavna, can we sit somewhere for some time? It's urgent. I'm leaving tomorrow and I want to tell you something," I requested.

"Hmm. Where shall we sit, Ajay?" she questioned.

"At Chhappan Bhog or any restaurant near Netram Chawraha."

'No, Ajay, I'm in my college uniform and it's late now. We can discuss it here, at the side of the road," she said, looking this way and that.

We walked next to the Allahabad University women's hostel; it was close to Prayag Station. Many other lovers were also standing there, and this made us feel quite comfortable.

"Bhavna, I'm leaving for good by the Shipra Express tomorrow."

"All the best for your future Ajay, and don't get disheartened because of Ragini," she said. But I could not focus on her words; I was up with my record player. "I have gathered some stuff. Bhavna, before leaving, I wanted to return all your things," I said and handed all her stuff to her.

"You kept all these things?" she replied quietly.

My lip stiffened. I handed her the snaps that were clicked during the freshers' party.

"Where did you manage to get all this?" she enquired. I remained silent.

"You can keep all these things. I'm perfectly fine with that."

My heart started beating faster and I felt choked up. I was sweating in February.

"Just coming, Bhavna," I said and went to a nearby tea stall. I gulped down some water and returned feeling like a warrior. Maybe Bhavna had understood by now.

I asked nervously, "Bhavna, I want to say something."

"Okay," she said, fearfully.

I summoned my courage and still staring at the ground, mumbled, "I love you, Bhavna."

"Come again?"

"I love you, Bhavna." I said with the same nervousness, but this time looking straight at my darling's face.

She was definitely not happy to see my eyes wet. She went silent; maybe she was still trying to digest the sudden admission of love.

"Ajay, you are a good friend, but I never thought of you in this way," she said, trying to console me. "Give me some time to answer.

But, don't be sad. You are a nice person, but I've never been in such a relationship before."

Then I realized the blunder I'd made. How could a girl accept a proposal when I still had a girlfriend? And tomorrow this lover boy was leaving college forever. I decided to correct the blunder.

"Bhavna, I have to tell you something about Ragini."

"What, Ajay?" she responded softly, so that I felt comfortable enough to share everything.

"I don't have an affair with Ragini."

"What?" She was aghast. "Then what's up with all those stories and photographs?"

"I made it up, so that you wouldn't keep yourself away from me. A person who is already in a relationship is surely considered safe." I sighed.

"Difficult to believe. Everyone knows about Ragini. Even Dipendra has shared things about her many times," she said confused.

"Ragini was one of my good friends at school. Nothing more. Bhavna, if you want, you can talk to her. She would love to talk to you."

"Does Ragini know about me?"

"Yes, on my visit to Rihand Nagar during the Diwali break, we talked about you."

I dialled Ragini's number and made Bhavna talk to her.

"Hi, Ragini. Ajay here."

"Hi, Ajay. How are you? And your story with Bhavna?" she asked.

"Ragini, I'm with her now. She wants to talk to you," I said and gave the phone to Bhavna.

What if Bhavna told Ragini those secrets that I had wanted to tell her during my school days but never had the courage to! It was a dangerous situation; my ex-crush was talking with my love-to-be – a rare moment in my life.

"Hi, Ragini."

"Hi, Bhavna. I've heard a lot about you. What's up?"

"Ragini, you and Ajay were never in a serious relationship?" Bhavna asked hesitantly.

"No, Bhavna. We are just good friends," Ragini answered.

The call ended after a few seconds of formal conversation. But Bhavna's actions had made me firmly believe that she also had feelings for me.

"Ajay, it's getting late. I have to go home. I need some time to think about all this."

"Bhavna, one last revelation for you," I said. I regained all my confidence and recovered from my sadness.

"Now what, Ajay? Enough for the day, I think."

I sighed, "Bhavna, I'm not going anywhere. I'll complete my degree in IERT."

"Why did you lie then?"

"Sorry, but this was the only way to get you here, so that we could talk."

"Will talk to you later," she said and left.

I kept standing there until my girl vanished into the darkness of the night. I started pedalling my Dreamliner cycle towards my hostel. Another war of thoughts began in my head. The positive part of me that said, Bhavna loved me, else she wouldn't have confirmed my relationship with Ragini. But the negative part of me said that Bhavna didn't love me, as she had left without accepting my proposal. Somehow, I felt the positive part winning. I felt relieved, like a huge burden had been suddenly removed from my head.

Breakup Day

14 February, Valentine's Day, 2004

I didn't go to college the next day, wanting to give an impression that I was depressed. I expected a sympathy call from Bhavna. It was like hoping for rain in Jaisalmer. I started plotting so that I could emotionally blackmail her. Yes, I was a bit sad, but was trying to project my fraud fracture as completely crushed.

Inside the hostel room, Gaurav was about to go to college.

"Gaurav I'm not well, yaar."

"What happened? You should consult a doctor," he said concerned.

"Nothing much, just viral fever. With severe body pain," I added.

"Your temperature is fine. It seems like something else", Gaurav felt my neck and wrist to check.

"Internal fever maybe."

"Consult a doctor," he suggested again.

"No, no. I'll be fine soon."

"Then, what do you want from me? My cock?" he asked, furiously.

'Listen, brother. If Bhavna asks for me, tell her that I'm not well and...and am not talking to anyone in the hostel." I called him 'brother' intentionally.

"Why, what happened? And what if she does not ask? Then?" he questioned.

I requested him, putting on a pitiful look, "Please understand, yaar. I'll feel nice if a caring person calls me. If Bhavna doesn't ask, then you still have to tell her this."

"Hmm," Gaurav said.

I pretended to cough again. "You can tell Beena as well. Please!"

"Buddy, please rest. The message will reach its destination," Gaurav assured me.

"Love you, yaar," I blinked with a cunning smile.

"Love, my ass! Saale tharki," Gaurav retaliated and left.

I had purposely not asked Dipendra to talk to Bhavna as he would have easily guessed that something had happened between us. By using all unfair means, dramas, emotions and blackmailing, I still didn't receive any call from Bhavna. My Valentine hadn't called me on Valentine's Day.

Bhavna had a badminton match on 15 February. I didn't shave that day in order to look like Devdas. I reached late. Bhavna's badminton match had already started, and after struggling, she eventually lost the match.

Bhavna, Beena, Gaurav and Dipendra were standing outside the court and were discussing the reasons for their loss. I was sitting at a distance and was busy pretending to be unwell. I was coughing like a dog. I had my own reasons for defeat. Bhavna came to me after five minutes. "Hi, Bhavna. Sorry about the result of the match," I said looking away from her. It was now difficult for me to look at her beautiful eyes.

"Yes, you should be. I didn't receive my friend's good wishes before the match."

"Sorry for being late. Actually, I wasn't well," I said and coughed again.

"Don't lie. Gaurav already told me that you are not talking to anyone in the hostel."

Love you, Gaurav, for hitting the mark, I mentally thanked Gaurav.

She continued, "Ajay, nothing has happened between us." I remained silent. "Nothing has changed, Ajay. You are still a good friend." For the first time, I hated the word 'friend'.

"From now, you are not going to bunk classes. And no more looking sad. I want my friend back...the way he was before."

She instructed me like a teacher and I nodded like an obedient student. I loved that she cared for me and at the same time I felt guilty for pretending. I decided not to do anything like that. If she loved me, she would accept me someday.

A few more days passed. The series of formal 'hellos' and 'byes' continued. I left everything to fate. No more emotional blackmail, no coughing, no more leaving my face unshaven. Nothing. I was lost in the recollections of the incredible Pioneer Computer class days and even cursed my luck sometimes.

21 February, 8.30 p.m.

My silver phone vibrated and the screen flashed, 'Bhavna Calling'.

"Hello, Ajay. Hope you are not busy. Can we talk?"

"Anything for you anytime, ma'am," I flirted.

"Listen carefully, Ajay. Please don't interrupt. Allow me to finish," she said rather seriously.

"If today anyone asks me who my best friend is, it's you," she sighed. "Even if anyone asks me who I like most, then it's still you."

I jumped in excitement and said, "What about....?"

"Wait...Don't poke your nose," she ordered.

"Yes, if anyone asks me, whom I love, I will say, 'Yes, I love Ajay.' Or, yes, I love you. But..." she sighed. This 'but' was killing me.

I remained silent.

"But...I don't understand this love. What I've understood is that you are more than my best buddy. Once we finish our engineering and settle into our respective lives, we'll definitely talk to our parents and marry. But till then, we'll be best friends, nothing more than that. I'm hanging up. We'll talk about this later."

Bhavna was not the kind of a girl to first fall in love, experience the relationship and then decide whether or not to marry. Love and marriage were the same thing for her.

"Wait," I pleaded.

"Not now. Today is my day," she said and disconnected the call.

That day, Jaisalmer became Cherrapunji and there was even a cloud burst. I was on cloud nine. I started dancing in my room, a customary drumbeat rolled internally and my mind started playing melodious music. This went on for the next fifteen minutes and I settled down on my bed, sweating badly. I could see the newspaper in which the love calendar was printed. I read it and began laughing uncontrollably; it was 21 February, Breakup Day.

Welcome to the crazy
world of love

Another name had been added to my list of good friends: Beena. People would see the three of us hanging out in the canteen, in the classroom, in labs, almost everywhere. We were an awesome threesome.

Beena always left college before Bhavna did. Like Bhavna, Beena was staying with her family as well. Beena was understanding enough to give Bhavna and me some space. Because of this, Bhavna and I had enough time together. Thanks for your generosity, Beena.

Yes, those were lovely days; and if you are in love, then nights are happier than days. The magical sound of violins seems to be playing all around you. I'd also been upgraded from my cycle to a Scooty. My Dreamliner was fighting the natural oxidation process of rusting. However, Bhavna's Scooty now had one more passenger. It became our chariot to explore the picturesque beauty outside our campus.

We had overcome the monotonous habit of saying 'hi' and 'bye' after two years. Now we were into exchanging some more romantic declarations such as 'love you' and 'miss you'.

The first year examination results were out. My girl stood 3rd, Akansha 2nd and Beena 8th. I also secured a rank, but it really doesn't seem worthy of mention. I was grateful that I had proposed to Bhavna before the exams results; she might have never agreed to be in a relationship after such a disaster.

The second year had also passed but I managed to keep my performance consistent. Bhavna had somehow managed the 3rd rank in class, which was a difficult task for a girl who spent most of the time in the canteen rather than in the labs. She used to offer her support and lend her notes not just to me, but also to my friends. By this time, my friends had become dependent on these notes and treated Bhavna like a guardian angel.

Bhavna used to share her concern and discuss our future and careers. But I never paid heed to her. I found myself lost in her beauty, which took my breath away.

I wanted to touch and feel her, but every time I attempted to steal a touch, she playfully stopped me with a blushing smile and said, "Control, Pandeyji, we are just more than friends." Listening to her 'Control Pandeyji', I always felt more uncontrollable. Sometimes I felt she was too idealistic, but that was the consequence of loving a saint.

Almost all my hostel friends had soul-mates now. Gaurav was in a relationship with Niharika, Dipendra started going around with Somya, and Arvind was with Kavita. Friends, you'll not believe this, but all of them are now happily married couples. Anyway, back to the story.

In February, during the fifth semester of our third year, Bhavna came to college with a pink nose. Whenever she cried, her nose turned pink. She looked pretty even while crying. I guessed easily that she had had a bad night. Twice she broke down into little sobs during the lecture. She avoided making eye contact with me to hide her tears. She made some excuses and went to the washroom. It really killed me to see her sobbing like that. I wanted to bunk the last lab but Beena wanted to attend it. So I left her to enjoy the circuits and signals.

Bhavna and I went into the college canteen. The canteen was the favourite hangout of all the lovers. It was the only place where lovers could spend many hours after ordering just a cup of tea worth three rupees. I did not know whether the uncle running the canteen was making money or not, but it was always house-full during our college days.

"What happened Bhavna?" I asked in a concerned tone. "I can't bear to see you like this."

"How much do you love me, Ajay! You always notice me," she said in a whisper-like soft voice.

"Thanks for understanding my love. Now may I know why my darling is so sad?" We had gone from being 'Ajay' and 'Bhavna' to 'sweetheart' and 'darling'.

She didn't say anything; her throat had choked up and her nose had turned red now. She was looking pretty, but it was not the time to be distracted by her alluring looks, so I said, concerned, "Feel free, dear. I'm up for anything."

She burst into tears and sobbed, "Ajay, I love you. I don't want to lose you."

Goosebumps covered my body. I asked, baffled, "So sweet, my darling. But, please, don't cry."

As I consoled her, I realized a bizarre fact of life; the more you request a girl not to cry, the more she will cry.

"My family is totally against love marriages and those kind of things," she said and sobbed again.

"Tell me in detail."

"Papa got to know about one of my close relative's affair and he proactively warned Pooja di and me, that he would not tolerate any such thing in our family. The situation at home is extremely awful."

She began wailing, again.

"Hold on, Bhavna. In between of all this, where is the question of leaving me?"

"Well ..." she said and started sobbing "...seeing things at home I'm thinking..."

"Go on, Bhavna. Spit everything out; I can understand what is going on inside you," I said, anxiously.

"Nothing could be more grievous and unfortunate for a parent than their child going against them," she said with great difficulty.

I desperately wanted to hug her, console her, but hugging in IERT was taboo. I said, holding her hand. "No need to say anything, Bhavna. I understand. You're thinking of sacrificing your love and relationship for your family."

"Sorry Ajay. Please try to understand me," she said.

What is there to understand? I don't know. I was puzzled. Sometimes her saintly behaviour made me faint.

"So this is a breakup meeting between us?" I questioned. She nodded with her eyes full of tears. "So, that was all your love for me."

My comment touched her heart. She replied, "I love you, Ajay. The tears that have been falling from my eyes are proof of that," she said gloomily. "Ajay, if we cannot sacrifice anything for our family, then we cannot love anyone."

I know I am biased for her, but her germs of being a good daughter always stop her from being a good girlfriend.

For a few seconds, I felt numb. So far I had only known how serious she was about me. So I could understand what she was feeling. But this decision of hers had earned her my immense respect. I decided I would never leave a girl who was so nice and ready to sacrifice her love for her family. I softly held her hand and pulled up her chin.

"Bhavna, you are an excellent daughter. Every family should have a daughter like..." I was about to finish but she cut me short without listening to me.

"Ajay, I don't have a brother. Our parents have always treated us like their sons. I can't ever leave them. Sorry, Ajay. But, leave me."

"How can I leave you when you are in trouble?" She frowned and I said, "I would have left you, if you were involved with someone. But I can't leave you during this tough time." I felt like a romantic hero.

These Hindi movies have spoiled many Romeos. "Now, answer me. If your parents can be convinced and they approve of our match, then would you mind marrying me?"

"If they agree, then it's gonna be the best day of my life," she said blissfully.

"So leave everything to me. I'll convince your father."

"Ajay, I know you are a persuasive person, but you don't know my family conditions."

"But, you know me."

"And my mother?" she said like she was a child negotiating for a toy.

"Yes. I'll convince your mother, too," I smiled.

"But how, Ajay? How...?"

Suddenly, Beena came into the canteen. She had also noticed that Bhavna had been tense. She had finished her lab work and had come to console her.

"Hi, Beena. Bhavna is asking me how I'll convince her parents about us," I grinned. As a third person arrived, the air changed. I realized that day that sometimes even couples shouldn't be left alone.

"As Bhavna already said, I'm the most persuasive person in the whole world. But she still wants me to explain how I'll convince her parents," I relayed to Beena.

Bhavna remained silent and to lift her mood I said, "Let's play a game. Beena, just pretend that you are Bhavna's father and I'm Ajay, Bhavna's husband-to-be coming to convince you to let me marry Bhavna."

Beena just settled down on the seat opposite me and Bhavna sat beside me. Beena and I acted out the scene. I requested, Beena, "Uncle, I'm here to marry your daughter. I love her a lot."

"Nowadays, I know children don't listen to their parents," Beena said. I watched her, aghast, hardly knowing what to say. Her statement seemed to have pained Bhavna even more.

"Uncle, I'm feeling hungry," I said to Beena.

"Oh Bhavna, *mehmaan aaya hai*...a guest has come home, please bring something to eat," Beena said. I made Bhavna bring us some cutlets. As Bhavna went to get them, I conspired with Beena.

"Beena, you have to get convinced easily. I'm not here to marry your daughter, okay?"

"Okay, Ajay. Understood," Beena whispered.

When Bhavna returned, we started up again.

"Uncle, please give me your daughter's hand, since I've all the qualities to ensure a good marriage. Apart from having a fair complexion, I already have a job and am moreover not going to ask you for a dowry. My proposal is totally free."

"Oh, free? Then why just her hand? Take all of her," Beena said.

Bhavna laughed. She looked amazing, her nose pink and her smile cute and dimpled.

❖

That same day, I spent some time talking to myself in the boys' hostel.

Mr Romeo Pandey, it took ten months to win Bhavna over. Convincing her parents would at least require a decade. And what about your parents who chant God's sermons all the times? For them, caste and religion are just like oxygen and blood. You'll need centuries to convince them about an inter-caste marriage. You're in for a lot of trouble, Mr Pandey. Welcome to the crazy world of love.

My struggle for placements

Almost all my friends had joined Professional Tutorial, a premier coaching institute for MBA preparations. Ironically, no one was interested in doing an MBA. They wanted to keep MBA as an alternate option, in case they failed to get a job through campus placements. As a blind follower, I joined the rat race.

With that, I had broken my old promise that I, Ajay Kumar Pandey, son of Sri Sri S.N. Pandey would not waste my family's wealth in coaching institutes.

That was not happening for the first time. I had broken many promises in the past, but lived up to one. You know what I mean. So let's focus on the forthcoming struggle.

Our third year of college was about to end. Bhavna's sister had happily married her boyfriend. Their family had agreed and blessed them. Her 'would be Jiju' had really become her Jiju now. Being a love marriage, it kick-started our hopes. These positive thoughts about our marriage strengthened the bond between us.

Bhavna also had a cell phone by then. But we talked little over the phone. We were not the kind of couple who woke up with 'Janu', 'Baby', 'Shona' and die moaning in pain and pleasure in the night. Bhavna used to bring two sets of everything: photocopied notes, almonds, assignments, and library books. We were a well-known couple in college now, and an inspiration to many. Everything was going smoothly. We were enjoying the quality time we spent together in college.

But this changed when this notice appeared on the college notice board:

First company for final year placements:
Satyam Computers Services Ltd.
Nodal Centre at UCER Allahabad.
First screening will be carried out via written examination followed by Group Discussion and HR interview.

This notice sucked away all our happiness. The whole college environment changed completely. Everyone geared up for the placements.

Being hostellers, we were more resourceful; everyone tried some kind of jugaad or trick. We got sample papers from *freshers.com* and the rest from the previous examination centres. We were all under the delusion that the written exam could be managed.

We got to the placement centre on D-Day; thousands of aspiring engineers were also present, looking like a flock of migrant Siberian birds. My stress increased when half a dozen buses arrived from different colleges. On seeing them, my hopes about the written examination were shattered and soon the pressure reached its peak.

I said to Bhavna and Beena, *"Meri to phat rahi hai.* I'm scared."

"I hate the slang you use, but *phat to meri bhi rahi hai,"* Bhavna said, tense.

"I'm sure I'm not going to clear it," Beena added.

We stared at the flock of students, who looked like Siberian birds for five minutes. Then I began to think about what jugaad or trick could be done. An idea flashed in my cunning mind.

"See girls, now we have to follow through with Operation Joint Effort." They frowned, but I continued, "The written test consists of fifteen questions and the duration is thirty minutes. So for every question, we have two minutes. All the questions can be managed, if there is no time restriction."

Both of them nodded like little kids.

I said pointing to Bhavna, "You start answering questions from the top and do the most you can do." And then pointing at Beena, "You have to start from the bottom, meaning the fifteenth question first, then the fourteenth and follow the same sequence. Remember you have five minutes for each question."

"In that case, do we just have to solve six questions?" Beena asked, puzzled.

"No, Beena. We'll work for twenty minutes, so four to five questions only."

"And what about the rest?" Beena asked. "What will you do?"

"I'll start from the middle. We'll have to finish this in twenty minutes and we'll exchange the answers using signs in the remaining ten minutes," I explained to them using my fingers as if I was teaching two dumb students.

Our mission was accomplished. Along with me, Bhavna, Beena, Dipendra and Arvind cleared the written examination and we entered the next gruelling session. The results were announced after two hours. Bhavna, Beena and I had cleared the group discussion round.

Now the most difficult task for us was waiting. The five page long pre-interview form was handed to us. It carried some basic information related to academics and hobbies.

Bhavna and Beena were tense. I had taken a mock interview of each of them and had asked them many predictable questions. I made suggestions and corrected them as if I had already given a hundred interviews.

The interviews went on till 9.00 p.m. All of us were exhausted. The final results would take a few hours. My head was aching. I requested Bhavna to come outside with me for some fresh air. Beena remained inside and would call us in case the results were announced.

We left the building and settled in a corner of the college garden. Only a few students were left. Those who could not make it to the following rounds had already left. The college looked far better than it had in the morning.

"Thank god, the Siberian birds returned to Siberia," I joked.

I lay down in the garden while Bhavna sat next to me.

"What happened, Ajay? Feeling tired?" Bhavna asked concerned.

"My head and legs are aching," I said, pressing my legs.

"I have a headache, too. But what is wrong with your legs? I have noticed that the bones in your legs seem to have a serious problem."

"Yes, dear. If I stand for two hours, they start aching."

"You should consult a doctor," she said massaging my head.

To avoid her excessive concern for my bones, I said, "Ma'am, just take a look around. It's such a romantic night. I'm lying in a garden and you are next to me at 9:30 p.m. Let's just feel it."

"Yes, you are right," she smiled.

"Bhavna, just imagine! What if we get into the same company in the same city?"

"Wow! It would just be a dream come true." Now her imagination awoke. "Software companies have two days off in a week. We'll enjoy every weekend and will have crazy parties. And when both of us are earning, then our parents will agree easily. We'll marry soon, and we'll stay together forever." Bhavna was in her own dream world. "And I'll send Aayushmaan and Pankhudi to you for mimicry shows."

"Who are Aayushmaan and Pankhudi?" I asked puzzled.

"Our kids," she blushed. It was unbelievable for me; it was not the age to discuss babies. But lovers do crazy things.

"What? You finalized this all by yourself? You didn't even feel the need to discuss this with me? And what if two boys or two girls are born?" I fired a string of questions at her.

"Then you will have the privilege of naming the second child," she said, pinching my cheeks.

Suddenly our series of romantic dreams were interrupted by a worried Beena. "Bhavna and Ajay, get inside! The results are out," Beena said.

The three of us assembled in the hall. I sat in the middle; Bhavna was to one side of me and Beena to the other side. A South Indian HR professional stood in front of us and began giving us unwanted gyaan.

"Dear engineers! Those whose names are not on this list are the lucky ones," he said waving a sheet of paper. "They should not feel bad, because they will get an opportunity to enter a better company than Satyam," he said as if he was himself ashamed of being Satyam's employee.

He continued giving us inspirational gyaan, but no one paid any heed to him. My heart started beating faster. I could hear every single heartbeat loud and clear, even through the deafening noise. I was worried; if he called my name, I would get a heart attack from being so happy. I started taking the name of every god. I was completely secular. I prayed to Allah, Jesus, Guru Nanak and every other god I remembered. I even prayed to the millions of Hindu gods, but it's possible that I said some devils' names in my hurry. Finally, after receiving unwanted gyaan for twenty minutes, the HR professional started calling out names. I looked at Bhavna. She had closed her eyes and was busy taking the names of the same gods. Then I realized that everyone around me was praying.

I thought, *god's bandwidth will get blocked today.* I whispered to god, *Please shift your network from the government to some private operator this time.*

Whenever a name was announced, it was followed by applause and cheers. Bhavna was still praying. She clutched my hand so tightly, it was as if she was in a hospital's labour room. It was the first time that Bhavna had held me like that. It was so romantic, but the fear was more powerful than the romance. It made me feel so emotional that I prayed again. "God, you never listen to me, but today, at least listen to her."

Then my beloved's name was announced: Bhavna Pradhan! She let go of my hand and joined the troop of selected students. After a few more names, another name was announced: Beena Mishra. She also left. I started cursing the same gods whom I had been begging a few minutes ago.

"Why me, every time, god? Why me? You should have at least considered Bhavna's request."

I remained seated and tears started rolling down my cheeks. *You should not be sad, Ajay. Your sad face will spoil her moment of victory,* I consoled myself. I collected myself since my darling had got her first job.

Everyone went outside after fifteen minutes. The air was filled with cheerful cries of 'I did it,' and 'Thank God,' and 'Love you.' Everyone was overwhelmed by their success.

Bhavna came to me, her nose pink and her eyes wet. As I looked deep into her eyes, both of us began to cry.

It was a rare moment. A girl was in tears after getting her first job, that too in a multinational software company. She was behaving as if she had lost everything. I could feel the intensity of the love and togetherness between us.

"Congratulations, dear," I said with a fake smile.

"Don't mention this crap and don't hide your emotions," she said firmly.

"Don't worry yaar. Didn't you listen to the HR fellow's gyaan? The people not selected are lucky. We'll get placed in better companies with hefty packages. And then you'll feel jealous."

She stared right into my eyes; I could see her eyes, not filled with water, but the pain was reflected in them. She said, "I can never be jealous of you, Ajay."

❖

The economy was booming in those days. Many software companies came to our campus. I was interviewed by about seven companies like TCS, Wipro, Infosys, HCL, L&T Infotech; they were all giants. But my luck never boomed. Fate cursed me every time.

Bhavna always wished me luck before every placement test, but god didn't have time for me. All my friends were placed, and my confidence was shattered. I felt completely broken. I didn't tell anyone at home about the placements, but since Dipendra and Arvind had been selected to join Infosys, everyone had already heard the news. The Common Admission Test results were out, but my bad luck continued. The CAT didn't change my luck.

I went home during the Holi break.

I lay on the bed, cursing myself. I remembered all the bad things in the past and blamed myself for all these unwelcome struggles. "Yes, I'm responsible for these failures. Yes, I'm a bad person and I deserve this."

My father came into my room, as I was busy demeaning myself. I pretended I was sleeping. He lay down next to me.

"Sonu," he prodded.

"Haan, Papa?"

"So how are the college placements?" he asked, touching my hair.

"Nothing much, Papa. Only Infosys turned up," I said, not mentioning all the other companies.

"Oh! You know, I was reading the newspaper. Infosys will be hiring twenty thousand people this year." I didn't respond. I was feeling dull, but my father was more than excited.

"Not to worry. TCS is planning to hire fifteen thousand and Wipro twelve thousand. And Satyam, too, is going to hire more than fifteen thousand."

I felt numb and cursed myself repeatedly. *These companies are hiring so many people and still you couldn't get into even one. Moron.* "Not to worry. Still three months to go...more companies will come to your campus, beta," my father said.

"Yes, I'm hopeful," I said.

"Not to worry, Beta. Don't feel low. Only one company has come for placements so far," he sighed. "It may be because Allahabad is far away from Bangalore and Pune."

I remained silent, feeling choked up. I was about to cry but somehow controlled myself. My father continued, "MBA fees are increasing day by day. What about your CAT results? If you get placed, will you still do an MBA?"

I lost all control and started weeping like a baby. My eyes became teary. My father hugged me and said, "Don't worry, my son. Don't worry about the MBA fees, beta. I'll manage the money if you want to do an MBA. I'll get some money from my provident fund. Please go ahead. But don't cry like this."

I cursed myself, *You are a bad son.*

I confessed while sobbing, "Papa all the companies that you just mentioned have already been to our campus, but your son could not even get into one."

"Don't worry, beta. Do an MBA. We'll mange everything," he said.

He kept hugging me and patting my back. But I didn't have courage to say that I had spoiled CAT as well.

❖

In April 2007, Bhavna wanted to go to the Mankameshwar temple in Allahabad. She had come to know that the presiding deity, Shanker Bhagvan or Lord Shiva, was powerful, and that his bandwidth was free for unfortunate people like me.

I accompanied her to the temple. She prayed silently but I could easily sense what she was asking for. I always understood her prayers; perhaps those were the only signals that I learnt to pick up during the four-year Electronic Engineering journey. I only prayed for god to listen to her. After winding up our begging session, we went to Saraswati Ghat on the banks of the Yamuna. You could see a panoramic view of the hanging Yamuna Bridge that was a famous attraction for tourists. If I could delete all the unwanted people from there, then it would become just a bay of heaven.

"When will the MAT results be out?" she enquired.

MAT was the other MBA entrance exam.

"Next week. It is my last hope," I sighed. Then I gave her a letter. "I wrote this. Just read, dear. I don't have courage to say anything," I said with a downcast face.

Bhavna,

I've always struggled in life. I never get anything easily. I struggled for two years to get into an IIT, but finally landed up at the IERT. I appeared for almost all the companies that came to college but you know the results. I even prepared hard for the MBA entrance, but that also seems like it might not turn out well for me. I always

try my best, but luck never takes my side. My confidence is crushed
and I have little courage to fight. I'm a big time loser and if you
stay with me, you'll also become a loser one day. If you feel that my
fortune has started affecting you, stop taking my calls for two days
and after that I'll stop calling you. I love you and I can't see my
beloved struggling along with me.

Love,
Ajay.

I thought she would explode at me after reading it but she said calmly, "Ajay, I'm keeping this letter in my bag and will show it to our kids, someday."

Whenever my emotions overpower me, I remain silent.

"Do you think all the idiots who were placed are better than you? Their luck favoured them; it's nothing like you can't do it. Let time pass and you will realize the same. Ajay, you are not an unfortunate man at all. Look... even after so many rejections, you haven't surrendered. You're still fighting." A lover's heart tried to find reasons to cheer me up despite her pain.

I remained silent. She went on. "Ajay, you want me to leave you for my happiness? Can anyone love me more than this?" she asked. "How can I leave you in trouble?"

She smiled, "Remember Ajay, when I was going through a bad time, was crying and had made a decision to leave you? What did you say? *'How can I leave you when you are in trouble?'* And today you are telling me to leave you," she paused. "Ajay, even if I die tomorrow and this is my last chance, I will say you are the best person in my life," she said with her eyes full of tears.

❖

In the hostel that night, while I lay on my bed, busy thinking about the future and Bhavna, suddenly my cell phone vibrated and I got a message from Bhavna.

There are two kinds of personalities.

There are those who have everything and still complain as if they have nothing. And there are those who lose everything and act like life has given them everything. Sometimes both these personalities exist in the same soul. Kill the first one, I love the second. And, yes. I love you and you are the best partner for me.

It's easy to make friends but difficult to keep them.

Tears welled up in my eyes and her loving, insightful and concerned message forced me to think.

What have I lost? Why did I cry in front of my father? I've such a loving family, and to add to that, I've such a loving partner. I cried over a job? No, Ajay, you can't cry for this. You are lucky to have such nice, supportive people around you.

This thought gave me a lot of hope. I texted her back that night at 12:30 a.m.

Love you, Bhavna, and I will never surrender.

Hyderabad to Pune

My MAT result was out after a few days. I managed to grasp a seat in a renowned MBA college, and to me that college was even better than the IIMs. I had two strong reasons for that – first, it has an extra M, its 'IIMM' (Indian Institute of Modern Management, Pune) second, it was Modern Management. As I did my engineering from Rural Technology, now I had moved to Modern Management. According to Bhavna, she had turned Rustic Pandeyji into Modern Pandeyji.

My amazing four years of engineering were finally over. In spite of craving for a job all the time, I could say those were the best days of my life. It had given me everything – true friends, good memories and an angel for a lifetime.

A year-and-a-half later, Bhavna had started working for Satyam Software Solutions Pvt. Ltd. in Hyderabad. I had completed three semesters of my MBA program from IIMM, Pune. This college offered a little extra in every aspect, whether it was the extra 'M' or some extra luck for me.

I received a job offer around Dusshera in 2008. The five-and-a-half years of frustration had somehow come to an end. The year-and-a-half apart had felt like a decade to us. Over this period, we talked on the phone for thirty minutes almost every day and for an hour on the weekends. We were grateful to Anil Dheerubhai Ambani and Reliance Communications who had made night calls free.

Being at IIMM was like being under military rule; it was compulsory to maintain a 95 % attendance record. As a result of this, I couldn't travel to meet Bhavna. So, Bhavna got on to the Hussain Sagar Express and came to Pune in the early morning hours of Diwali.

During the wee hours of Diwali morning, I was at the Pune railway station. I was excited because the Hussain Sagar Express was about to arrive. Even though it was one in the morning, I was not sleepy. It was the first time I had bought a bouquet of flowers for her. As I reached the platform, I saw one of the drivers holding a sign with the name 'Dr Astha' on it.

I had a shrewd idea.

There were many advertisement flyers pasted around the platform; they had colourful pictures on one side and were blank on the other. I peeled a flyer off, hoping to write something on its blank side, but at 1:15 a.m, I couldn't find anything to write with. I saw a lady sitting close by, applying some lipstick. Ladies seem to be able to use make up at any given moment of the day. Gathering all my courage, I went to her and said, "Namaste, aunty."

She stared at me; calling a lady 'Aunty' is the biggest sin one can commit. I corrected myself quickly. "Sorry, ma'am. The problem is that my boss is coming and I forgot to bring a sign with me. My cell phone is also not working."

"I'm not going to give a stranger my cell phone," she interrupted to say.

"Oh, sorry, aunty... I mean, ma'am. I don't want your cell phone. I want to write something on this. May I use your lipstick, please?" I grinned. But the word 'please' became helpless to please her.

"Hello, mister! It's L'Oreal," she said like I had requested her for her entire wealth. She gave me a dirty look.

"Okay, no issues," I sat down beside her, pretending to look sad. She looked at my bouquet and as ladies are known for their kindness, she saw my fake cow expression and melted.

"I can give you my pencil. But give the paper to me, I'll write for you."

Pencil? Is she a teacher or student keeping a pencil in her bag, I thought.

She opened her purse and I peeped inside. There were numerous bottles, some tubes, a mirror, a brush and many more things. I felt sorry for the bag. After looking through what felt like an ocean, she took out her eyeliner. I was a bit surprised to see the crazy number of beauty products ladies use and wondered if Bhavna used these products as well?

"Tell me the name," she asked.

I thought for a second and said, "Mrs Pandey. Boss' wife."

The train arrived at the platform after five minutes, and I received a call from Bhavna. "Ajay, your darling has arrived at the platform. Where are you?" she said excitedly.

"Please look around the platform. You'll find me," I disconnected the call. The lady beside me looked at me as if I was a terrorist and mumbled, "Your cell phone was not working?"

I didn't say anything to her. I was busy welcoming my darling who was coming to me after a long time. But this Bhavna was different. She wore a white top with blue jeans, her short hair had grown eight inches longer, the spectacles were gone and a lovely bindi adorned her forehead. As she came closer, I realized that it was not a bindi, but a mole. It was like god had adorned her forehead for me. Things like this happen when love birds meet after a long gap.

I had never noticed the mole in the centre of her forehead before; maybe it hadn't been noticeable. I wondered if god had decorated my Kajol. Seeing the sign I had made, she came to me, kissed it all over and hugged me. Hugging in Pune is more acceptable than in Allahabad.

When lovers meet after a long time, they tend to do certain things in public, so keep meeting regularly if you wish to avoid this. I gave her the bouquet and she smelled it like it was the most precious perfume.

"Missed you a lot, dear," Bhavna said. Even though she had been travelling by a wait-listed ticket, she showed no sign of tiredness.

"Happy Diwali, darling," I said.

"This is the happiest Diwali, Ajay," she responded and pinched my cheek.

The lady, who had lent me her eyeliner, continued staring at us like she was going to swallow me up. Her lipstick seemed to have vanished from her lips in her anger. She kept throwing us dirty looks and her lips formed the words, "Your boss?"

"This is Mrs Pandey and she is my boss," I answered. My next words added fuel to the fire. "Thanks and bye, aunty."

We left quickly.

I had made arrangements for Bhavna to stay in the girl's hostel. I started my friend's bike and headed towards Wakad. My boss sat behind me on the bike and smelled the flowers.

"Which lipstick did you use in the college?" I asked Bhavna while driving.

"What? Are you nuts? I never used any lipstick in college. You never noticed that?" she said. Then I realized I had committed a sin again.

"Well your lips are always red. I thought you might have used some lipstick," I defended myself and changed the subject to something less dangerous.

"Wow! Look, the Pune weather is so cool and everything looks awesome because of Diwali."

But girls are girls and Bhavna said, "I've heard a lot about Pune girls and especially the IIMM girls. Is this lipstick subject about them?"

I sighed and explained everything to her.

Thirty minutes later, we were nearing Aundh, when it suddenly started pouring cats and dogs. Pune rain is unpredictable. I parked my bike under the shade of a tree. We settled in a corner under the tree. The weather was cool and a biting wind was blowing. There was a car parked near us. We noticed that a couple was kissing inside the car. Kissing was not the right word for them; they seemed to be eating each other up.

The rain was not stopping. I looked at my bike.

"I wish I had a car," I cursed and sighed.

"What is this, Ajay? You always cursed your cycle, now you are cursing this bike, too?"

"Kissing in a car is much better than kissing out on an open road."

"You're a big idiot. You never appreciate what life has given you," she said. She stretched both her hands to the sky, and walked out from the shade.

"Look, it's such a beautiful Diwali night. The rain is welcoming me and I'm with the best person in the world."

How could I stop myself from going out into the rain? We were completely drenched. Bhavna said, "Please, sing a song, Ajay."

I didn't want to disappoint her with my horrible voice. I pulled out my phone and searched for a song. I put the phone in a plastic bag so that the rain wouldn't spoil it.

'Aaoge jab tum saajana, angna phool khilenge,
Barsega saawan jhoom jhoom ke, do dil aise milenge.'

The song was from Bhavna's favourite movie, *Jab We Met*.

Bhavna started swaying on the side of the road. I found Pune very romantic for the first time and Bhavna's love for the rain was a catalyst to this romance. We were completely drenched. I started the bike as there was no point waiting in the shade.

I changed the words of the song to suit her and we sung it together.

'Aaoge jab tum, Bhavna, angna phool khilenge,
Barsega saawan jhoom jhoom ke, do dil phir se milenge.'

❖

IIMM was the only college that had classes all year round. There were no holidays, so the college always made arrangements to celebrate each festival. Hence, a big firecracker display had been organized on the campus. When we reached IIMM, I asked Bhavna, "So ma'am, what did you bring for me?" I used to address her as ma'am, maybe we were going beyond the boundary of cupid lovers.

"Yes, I've two things for you. One, biscuits from Karachi Bakery," she said, handing a packet to me.

I opened it like a hungry monster, when half a cookie was in my mouth and other half hanging from my mouth, she said, "And the second gift..."

She gave me a torn letter.

I opened the letter. It was the same letter I'd written to her, when I was disappointed after a number of rejections during placements and was thinking about ending our relationship. I fell silent.

"Mr Ajay, do you still believe this?"

"No. But this is not fair. You said that you would show this to our kids."

She held my face in her hands and said, "Ajay, please remember your words; never give up. And please follow this in your life, okay?"

she said acting like a teacher. I loved that I had such a lovely teacher in my life.

"Ok, ma'am," I responded like an obedient student.

❖

We were sitting in the college cafeteria and Bhavna had opened a packet of biscuits from Karachi Bakery.

"You have been eating biscuits like a panda for the last five minutes. Share with your friends, too," Bhavna said. "You are a true Brahmin."

"Don't curse me, ma'am. Tomorrow you will also become a Brahmin," I said. She blushed. Anything related to marriage excited her.

"Who are your MBA friends?"she asked.

"Amit, Mohsin and Vaibhav."

"You borrowed the bike last night from Vaibhav?" she asked.

"Yes. Good friend."

"He was the same one, who had some matchmaking problem?"

"Yes. The age old problem of our Indian society; the inter-caste marriage. He is Brahmin and the girl is from another caste."

"You are also a Brahmin."

"Bhavna, please! I get goosebumps when someone reminds me that I'm a Brahmin."

As we sat in the canteen, we rated the beautiful college girls. There was no sign of the Diwali spirit. It felt more like a fashion show was about to start. A few girls were wearing sleeveless tops, a few were in miniskirts and micro-minis, backless tops, and half shoulder tops with deep necklines. The show went on. On the other hand, a poor girl in jeans had come all the way from Hyderabad. She watched it open-mouthed.

"Ma'am, at least close your mouth or one of these girls will jump inside."

"Pune girls are really hot. You're still a... you know na?" she joked. We both laughed.

"So Ajay, how is your MBA experience? Have you applied any management principles to your real life?" She kept the conversation rolling so that my eyes could not roll over other girls. The presence of a girlfriend can help you focus even in such distracting situations.

"Problems are opportunities," I said.

"What is this crap?" she asked.

"I only remember this quote; Bala Sir, my college director, sang the same old song throughout the year."

"This is really disgusting. First, he creates a problem for you and then he asks you to figure out the hidden opportunity in it?" Bhavna said, angry over my not getting a Diwali holiday.

"Don't worry, ma'am; there is an opportunity here to see a good fireworks show."

We both proceeded towards the firecracker display which was organized over the open ground. I saw two hot girls approaching me; both waved as they drew closer to me.

Juhi shouted, "Happy Diwali, Ajay!" She gave me a hug. In spite of enjoying that opportunity, I turned my face to gauge the problem, I grinned broadly. Bhavna's dimple endowed cheeks were totally round and it was like someone had blasted an atom bomb over her head. And then it turned into a serial blast when the second girl also hugged me.

I grinned and said, "Happy Diwali! Meet my girlfriend and would be wife, Bhavna." I said 'wife' so that the intensity of Bhavna's blast of anger would decrease.

"Happy Diwali, to both of you," Bhavna said half-heartedly.

Juhi understood the situation. She sighed and said. "Pandeyji, problems are opportunity."

That day, I realized a weird fact of life, if your name is followed by Pandey, then no one will call you by your first name. You will be known as Pandeyji.

Both left and now the calf was left alone with the tigress.

"Just friends," I grinned.

"Pune girls are really lewd! If this is happening in front of me, what could be happening behind my back? And why is the whole world calling you Pandeyji?"

"They love me," I dropped another bomb by mentioning the word love.

"They love you," she repeated, giving me a dirty look.

"They love me as a friend," I said aghast.

"And hug you like a brother?" She looked straight into my eyes.

"See Bhavna, it's just a daily thing for them and..." I continued looking for mercy, but she started laughing. Girls are weird like that. They laugh at anything.

She cut in and said, "Ajay, I'm just kidding. I know you. But I feel jealous if someone hugs you." The emotional drama went on for another ten minutes.

Suddenly, one more female friend came in. I folded my arms so that Avineet would not jump and hug me.

"Happy Diwali, Avineet. Meet Bhavna," I mentioned Bhavna intentionally.

"Happy Diwali, Bhavna. So, Mr Pandeyji, now that your girlfriend is here, you are not even going to hug me?" Avineet said.

Bhavna glared like the hot sun glaring down on the desert. Suddenly the firecracker display started with a bang. The whole college was busy watching the display. But the show had begun fifteen minutes before time for me, and continued for another half an hour.

Pune to Mumbai

It was time for Bhavna to go back. We had reached the Pune station.

"Hussain Sagar Express; which platform?" I asked a coolie dressed in red.

"Where do you want to go?" he asked.

"How does it matter to you? Just tell me if you know," I responded unpleasantly.

"Platform number four," he said and left.

We found a seat on the platform and waited for the train. *I hope this train is indefinitely delayed*, I put my arm around Bhavna's shoulder.

"Ajay, my parents are forcing me to look for a groom. I have to tell them about us soon. What are your plans for marriage?" she asked.

"They are not going to wait for your part-time MBA to get over?"

"That was a lie to buy time. Now they know that I'm not interested in an MBA. I can delay it for one year at the most."

"Yaar, I've not joined the company yet. And I need at least two years to settle into my career, after which we can get married."

"Then marry one of the girls who were hugging you in your college. My parents are not going to wait for more than a year," she said firmly. "And they'll not wait for my permission to start looking for prospective grooms."

"Let them start the hunt. The moment they find a groom for you, tell them about me."

"Mr Ajay Kumar Pandey. First of all, you commit to me that you'll convince my parents."

"Ok, dear. I'll talk to your parents."

"Ajay, if any IAS or PCS offers come, they'll start comparing you to them. Then convincing my parents will be an impossible task for you," she said and the image of an IAS or PCS villain came to my mind. At that moment, all unmarried government officers seemed disgusting to me.

"Okay listen, yaar. First, I'll tell my parents and then yours. Please give me at least six months to breathe," I sighed but the angel seemed to have turned into a demon.

"Ajay, one thing should be clear; I can't leave my family under any circumstance. I will remain unmarried my whole life, but I'll not go against them. In short, *main bhaag kar shaadi nahi karoongi.*"

"*Bhaag kar*? No one runs during weddings."

"Can we talk seriously?" she said as if we had been pretending to be Tom and Jerry for the last twenty minutes.

"Don't talk seriously. I'll get a heart attack."

"Ajay, I know you can convince them."

"How do you know that I can? Even I'm not sure about it as yet." I sighed. Meanwhile, the train arrived.

You also sometimes behave like God who never listens to me, I cursed the Indian railways.

"Bhavna, please don't go, yaar. You were just here for twenty-four hours," I said.

"Ajay, don't say things like this. You know how I got this reservation. I can't help it." We hugged and parted with heavy hearts.

I went back to my room and fell asleep at around three in the morning. The next morning at six, I was sleeping peacefully. But my sleep was disturbed by the ringing of my phone. When I tried to pick it up, it got disconnected.

"Who the hell is this, calling me so early?" I yelled, half in my sleep.

I yawned and opened one eye to look. The screen showed seventeen missed calls from a landline number. I was shocked.

Had something happened to Bhavna? Suddenly it rang again. I picked it up.

"Ajay, I'm in Mumbai," Bhavna cried. She was sobbing like a little child.

"Mumbai! How?" I found I was wide awake.

"I don't know. Wrong train I think," she said, sobbing harder.

"Okay. Okay, control yourself, Bhavna. Do one thing. Just buy a local ticket and sit in the ladies' compartment and come to Pune. I'll manage the rest."

"Okay, I'll try, Ajay. Missing you."

"Missing you, too. But remember, Bhavna...every problem is an opportunity," I said.

"Where is the opportunity in this?"

"Okay, forget that. Just follow my instructions."

I surfed the internet and tried to figure it out. There were two trains with the name Hussain Sagar Express. Both depart from Pune. One departs at 1:15 a.m. for Mumbai and another at 1:25 a.m. for Hyderabad. They go in two different directions.

My phone rang again.

"Ajay, there is a long queue. I can't buy a ticket." She was sobbing, again.

"Listen Bhavna," I said and I explained. "What has happened to your phone?"

"It's not working. Maybe it was damaged in the rain that night."

"No need to panic. I'm coming to Mumbai right away. I can't call on your number, you have to call me after three hours. Okay? Understood?"

As I said that, I felt I was behaving like a teacher.

"Okay."

"Till that time, please be cool and don't panic."

I took my driving license and got ready to leave for Mumbai. But because of only three hours of sleep, my eyes closed every few minutes. I drove half a kilometre and almost fell asleep twice during that time. I started getting goosebumps. I parked my bike on the side of the road and tried to fight against my own body. I splashed gallons of water on my face and started mumbling angrily, "Never surrender Ajay, never surrender."

But my eyes were surrendering and I prayed, *Oh, God please help me.* My phone vibrated. An unknown landline number was calling.

"Ajay, I got the ticket. A police uncle helped me."

"I'll see you at Pune station. But your phone is not working. How am I going to know when you reach the station?" I asked. I appreciated that my mind was not as sleepy as my eyes.

"I'm coming by the local train. It starts at nine and will be reaching in three hours or so. Look around for me at the time of arrival," she suggested.

"Love you, dear. And I'm definitely going to be on the platform."

Two local trains were coming to Pune station from Mumbai at twelve o'clock. One was coming from Kalyaan and the second from Mumbai. When the train arrived, I found the world's most beautiful face, but the magical smile was missing from her face. I sighed in relief. Bhavna came and hugged me like never before. She didn't say anything. Only tears rolled down her cheeks for a few moments.

"Every problem is an opportunity," I whispered.

"What is the opportunity here?"she murmured.

"The opportunity to see you again," I said while breaking free of her grip.

"*Sadiyal kahin ke*. You idiot."

And the rain began to fall again. I sang *Aaoge jab tum*, changing the lyrics to suit our situation.

'*Aaoge jab tum, Bhavna, angna phool khilenge,*
Barsega saawan jhoom jhoom ke, do dil phir se milenge.'

Winning half the battle

One year later, 2009

The day I joined Redington India limited, Bhavna was given a sabbatical from Satyam Software Company. A huge corporate scandal had surfaced after a public announcement by the company's CEO. But she was called back after six months. There had been many similar incidents that took place during that time, but let's focus on the herculean task of my life: my struggle to marry Bhavna.

Bhavna's father had been transferred from Allahabad to Raipur. Bhavna was still in Hyderabad working for Satyam and I'd shifted to Delhi and started living in the East of Kailash. The distance between us had increased, but our hearts remained united. We found that the nights proved to be the best and the most soothing time for us to talk. We chatted daily on the phone and now Pandeyji, the all-time struggler, was no longer jobless. All my phone bills were now sponsored by Redington India Ltd. After settling into our respective jobs, we started setting the stage to discuss our love marriage in our respective homes. During the course of the execution of the biggest plan, all news related to suicide, divorce and dowry cases of arranged marriages were portrayed well in front of the families.

November 2009

Bhavna gave me a missed call. My phone bill was funded by my company, so it became my moral duty to call her back.

"Hi, sweetheart. How was your day?" I asked, for frequent callers the word 'hello' seems hollow sometimes.

"It was good, Ajay," she replied in a low voice. "Ajay, I'm not getting any calls from companies in Delhi."

"Have patience, darling. Patience always bears sweet fruits." When men don't have answers, they philosophize.

"What sweet, yaar. We've not been together for the last three years and my family is behind me.'

"Behind you! For what?" I asked, hoping she was not participating in a marathon.

"A twenty-six-year-old girl, with a job, settled but still unmarried," she said. Girls never talk about their ages; once they mention their age, it means the age old drama will start.

"Okay, don't start again."

"Ajay, you are the biggest phattu...such a coward. You've been trying to tell your parents about us for the last six months."

"Bhavna, I'll definitely discuss us within one year. And moreover, I'm telling them the advantages of love marriages every day."

"Ajayyy! Keep that advantage of yours in your pocket and listen to me," she said in a serious tone and I remained silent. 'Ajayyy' was always a dangerous word. When Bhavna said it, it meant the situation was serious and no more pranks or PJs would be tolerated.

"I love you dear," I said slyly, smelling the danger. But she ignored my declaration.

"Today, Mummy was asking for my permission to start hunting for a groom. She might have a suspicion that I'm in a relationship," she said.

"You are lucky. At least your mother is asking for your consent."

"Yours?" she asked.

"They declare their verdicts: hang with a Brahmin girl until your death."

"Ajay, don't frustrate me," she said. It was my family and my problem, but she was getting unnecessarily frustrated.

"Okay, okay, so, how did this give you the idea that your mother is aware of our chemistry?" I changed the topic.

"I don't know about chemistry or biology, but the next time Mummy asks, I'm definitely going to tell her first. Then I don't care if you want to tell your family first."

"Bhavna, please understand. I'll need some time to convince my family. Maybe one year or more. If you tell your family first then I'll have to convince my family within a limited time. After that, your mummy will start asking feedback about my family's stand on this marriage issue every day."

"Mr Ajay, what do you think? My father is Amrish Puri from *DDLJ*? I'll tell him today that I like Shahrukh Khan and he will say, '*Ja, jee le apni zindagi*'," she mimicked an actor from the film. Normally I'm the one who mimics, but love always brings out something new and refreshing in each partner.

"Okay, give me three months, ma'am. I'll definitely tell them."

"Take six months, Ajay." I felt a bit happier and was trying to understand whether I'd heard her correctly or not. She continued like a Supreme Court judge.

"In these six months, you have to convince them about the marriage."

We talked for another fifteen minutes and said we loved and missed each other and wished each other sweet dreams. But there was no sweetness in my dreams. I went to my cupboard and looked for a picture of Bhavna. I had a million pictures of her, maybe more than she had of herself. I found a photo of hers with short hair and I kept it in my wallet, saying "You looked so cute with short hair. Why did you change your hair style? You look more dangerous now." I smiled, then said, "But I loved you then, and I love you now."

❖

I got a call from the most known number the next day. Please note that it was not a missed call. I was slightly busy and cut the call thinking I would call her after finishing my work, but she called again. I cut the call and called her back.

"Do you have spicy news?"

"How did you know that I have something to share?" she said, brightly.

"First give me the good news."

"I've done too much, Ajay," she said in a loud voice.

"What? You revealed our relationship?"

"Yes, Pandeyji! Muah!"

"And, let me guess. They agreed."

"I love you, Ajay. You know me the best." I smiled and wondered if this was a problem for every beautiful girl.

"Can I get the details from the cheerful girl?" I asked.

"As usual, Mummy called me and said that they were planning to upload my profile on a matrimonial site. She said they were totally comfortable if I wanted to discuss anyone I liked with them. They said, they didn't want any drama later on. I said no initially, but it sounded completely hollow. So she probed again, I again said no, but this no was somewhat yes for her, she probed again, 'Bhavna, you are a mature girl,' she said."

"Then you fired the gun of immaturity," I guessed.

"Don't poke your nose when I'm speaking." And she went on, "Mummy had already met you at Pooja di's wedding. She remembered your face and asked what were you doing? Then I dangled the carrot: an MBA graduate, working as a manager in an MNC, father has a government job as a Senior Engineer and belongs to a Brahmin family. Then after a minute of ifs and buts, she said that they were okay with you."

We do MBAs for many reasons in India. Finally, my MBA degree was utilized for the right purpose.

"You lied about my father. He is a Junior Engineer."

"It hardly matters to them. Only you matter," she said.

This reminded me of the time I'd promoted my father from Junior Engineer to Engineer; and today his would be daughter-in-law had promoted him to Senior Engineer. *Congratulations for your out of turn promotions, Papa. If it goes on like this, you'll definitely become the Managing Director of NTPC one day.*

She interrupted my chain of thought, "Ajay, I've done my part. Now, it's your turn," she sighed.

"Yes, it's a great relief. We have won half the battle, at least," I sighed.

"But..." she said.

"Yeah, tell me. I know there is always a 'but' in my life. I never get anything easily. So spit it out," I sighed, again.

"But my family is only interested in an arranged marriage. No elopement."

"Yeah. It's against my belief system too," I said like the hero of a flopped Hindi movie.

"Love you, my Shahrukh."

"Love you, my Kajol," I flirted.

"But Shahrukh is married to Gauri."

"But Kajol is married to Ajay. You just remove 'Dev' from 'Devgan' and everything is the same. I even have a gun."

"Mr Tharki Pandey, in college you'd committed that you would convince my family. Look, I've done fifty percent of your work. Now please be quick about your part."

Girls always remember one-sided commitments. I said something but she was busy dreaming about our marriage and busy listening to the *shehnayi*. But I was imagining my family's scary questions. I didn't know when we would be able to hear shehnayi in reality.

❖

Bhavna called me the next day.

"Ajay, Mummy was asking me when you are going to talk to your parents," she said. It was expected now, that every day, the same anthem would be heard.

"What did you say?"

"I asked for another four months for you. I said that when you go home during Holi, you will definitely discuss it."

She stressed on the words 'four months' as if she had given me four years.

"I knew this would happen."

"What? Have I done anything wrong?"

"No, Bhavna you haven't. Listen, now onwards, whatever I tell you to reveal, you have to vomit that only," I said.

"So weird," she said.

"Bhavna, your parents are probably thinking that Mr Ajay Pandey will go home and reveal everything about you and the very next day or maybe in a week's time both families will be able to start booking marriage halls."

"Ajay, I understand. I'll not reveal any additional information," she said.

"Give me some time to think. Will let you know the next piece of news you can share."

After the chat, I lay down on my bed and started thinking about the most frightening possibilities.

How to tell my family about Bhavna? Should I talk to my mother or father first? Bhavna's parents will not listen to anything after Holi.

My mind was muddled with unfolding thoughts. I suggested to myself, *Mr Ajay Pandey, the more you delay this, the more tense you will be. It's better to die in one go rather than poison yourself a little every day.* I went to the IRCTC website and booked a ticket for a round trip on the Prayag Raj Express. I picked one notebook and started writing in my Chinese writing.

I called Bhavna the next day.

"Bhavna, on Friday night I'll be going to Naini in Allahabad to meet my parents. They are at Tauji's place."

"So, are you going for us?" she asked.

"No, Bhavna. I'm going for myself, since I can't procrastinate anymore," I sighed. "Bhavna, I've written a letter to my father. I don't have the courage to say anything aloud."

"So, your father is going to receive a letter bomb?" She asked, seriously.

"First listen to my letter, Bhavna."

Dear Papa,

Sorry for always troubling you. I know I'm not a good son, but I love you and Maa a lot and I understand my responsibilities too. So, in order to fulfil each and every responsibility of life, one needs to be with the right partner. Choosing a life partner is the most important decision for a human being. If someone has the best better half, then he'll surely succeed in life. This important decision should be made by the person whose life it is. I know someone who is mature and caring and is perfectly suited to me. Her name is Bhavna.

I know Bhavna doesn't belong to our caste and this will be a matter of worry for you. But I can't leave the best person only because she was not born in the womb of a Brahmin. She is not at all responsible for her birth, neither am I responsible for mine.

Every person has his or her own ideology about life that gives them confidence. Brahmin and Kayastha is not a digesting reason for me. If I leave Bhavna for such a silly reason, it would ruin my faith in life. It's possible that I could start cursing myself and you. And at the end of the day, no one would win. I know that only a happy person can inspire others to be happy. Every parent wants to see their kids happy and my happiness is only with her. I feel lucky to have the world's most loving father. I hope you understand your son's love.

Your troublesome son,
Sonu.

After reading it aloud, I found it difficult to talk, as my heart was burdened with guilt, and tears welled up in my eyes. Bhavna was silent for a few seconds and after regaining her voice she said, "Ajay, I love you."

I didn't say anything and Bhavna realized what I was feeling. I disconnected the call and texted her:

Will talk later. Love u. I'm fine.

Only love makes us realize that we all are good in some way. The text I got in response read: *Believe me Ajay, you are a good son.*

My first tsunami

I was at Naini in Allahabad at my grandparents' house where my Tauji lived. My parents had come to Naini to attend a wedding. I had not slept a wink the entire journey and thought about all the reasons I could give for the anticipated resistance. Instances of my parents' support and love flashed in my mind every minute. Why had I fallen in love, I asked myself a million times, but every time her image cleared my doubts. I reached Naini at around 9.00 a.m. I slept through the day and remained silent but there was a storm inside me.

That evening at around seven, I called my energy booster.

"Hello, Ajay."

"Yaar, *meri to phat rahi hai.*" I responded ignoring her hello.

"I can understand. Don't feel bad about anything. Just go and tell them all the positive things about my family. And that we are also vegetarian, I believe in God and pray for at least hundred minutes every day."

"Do you really pray so much?"

"Oh, my baby." For the first time, I used the word 'baby' to address her. "Why aren't you a Brahmin, Bhavna?"

"But a Kayastha is not very low."

"Bhavna, you don't know yaar. They believe they are born Brahmin, because of their good karma in their previous births. Even when the marriage is arranged within the same caste, they evaluate whether the other family is upper caste Brahmins or lower caste Brahmins."

"What?" She exclaimed, shocked. "Brahmins have sub-castes also?"

"Yes, and for details on the subject, you'll have to pursue another engineering degree in Brahmin Technology. And even then I'm not sure if you'll pass or not."

"May I know if you belong to an upper sub caste or a lower one?" she asked inquisitively to know her own status.

"I don't belong to any caste. I only belong to you," I said. Love makes a person secular. "Bhavna, I've to go."

"All the best and remember, problems are opportunities."

I smiled and said, "Such a loving opportunity."

❖

My father was planning to leave for the wedding as my mother had to accompany the other ladies. I forced myself. *Ajay, this is the best time to talk to Papa.*

"Papa, may I come along with you for the wedding?"

I rarely attended any wedding function. He was surprised. He gave me a look and said, "Get ready fast. I'm waiting." After five minutes, we took the scooter and headed to the wedding venue. Meanwhile, Papa asked the usual questions. I gave short and one-line responses.

I tried to tell him twice, but failed. When we reached close to the venue, Papa began searching for a parking space. I pulled my wallet from my back pocket, kissed the photo, and said silently, "I love you, dear opportunity," and started murmuring, "Never surrender, Ajay..."

Papa parked the scooter and started walking towards the banquet hall. I stopped him and handed him the letter. "Papa, a letter for you," I said, and not knowing why, my eyes got moist. It could have been the guilt for hurting him washing over me.

"Why are you crying, beta? Please tell me frankly," he said softly. It was an unexpected response from him. Parents always understand us, sometime even more than we understand ourselves.

"I've written everything in the letter," I said. He opened it, but his eyes were fifty years old.

"Can't read. I forgot my spectacles at home. Now, please tell me what the matter is?" He surrendered against my seemingly Chinese handwriting. Gathering all my courage, I was able to speak.

"Papa, the girl who came for didi's wedding..." I found that my throat was choked but this was enough for a loving father like him.

"Bhavna?" He said my favourite name. I nodded.

A short silence fell for a few seconds and he broke it in a worried tone, "She belongs to another caste, beta."

❖

At noon the next day, I was still buried under the covers of my bed, when Mummy called me.

"Sonu, please come outside."

Naini was quite cool in December. And after the tsunami had occurred, everything felt colder. I settled down on the bed with my mother on one side and my father on the other. The situation had become tense. Their eyes were red; they must have been crying.

"Sonu, you are an intelligent boy. How did you do this?" My mother took her first shot. I remained silent. That was the trap. If someone says that you are intelligent, it means you are dumb.

"Son, if I agree to your decision, I'll be rejected by all my brothers and family members. All my social relationships will be ruined," Papa said as Maa started weeping.

"Beta, you are such an obedient son. You have to forget her," she said sobbing. Tears started falling from my eyes. I was hundred percent sure that I'd not been doing anything wrong. But it's unbearable to see your caring parents crying in front of you and to know that you are the reason for their tears.

"But Maa, what is the logic in it? Why should I leave her? You didn't even ask what she is doing. What her family is like! You're telling me to leave her because of other people who don't even matter to me," I said softly.

"Bhavna's parents are aware of all this?" Papa asked. My father always asks logical questions.

"Yes, they have no problems. But they agreed on a condition: they'll only support us when both our parents agree to this," I said. This increased my parents' determination.

"Why would *they* have a problem?" Maa said with pride.

"Maa, have you ever seen a couple from different castes who had an arranged marriage? Each individual respects the other's caste. If someone says yes for an inter-caste marriage, it means they respect their daughter's feelings more than their religion or caste," I said in a low voice.

"No one would marry your brother," Maa said. This frustrated me. Now, my brother was unnecessarily being portrayed to me as a villain.

"Maa, we are living in modern times. What are you talking about? Maa, I should leave her for the society since no one will marry my siblings. Society has never helped anyone; whether you do something right or wrong, it only criticizes," I said and my mother cried again.

I went on, "Sorry for troubling you, Maa and Papa. I know she is the best match for me. You can't find anyone better than her."

"Sonu, give me Bhavna's number. I'll talk to her and will try to explain our situation," Papa said gently.

"Don't talk to her Papa. She'll leave me if I even text her." I felt a lump in my throat; my mother handed me a glass of water.

"She only told me that if you do not agree, don't hesitate to leave me," I said with great difficulty.

My mother hugged me and kissed my forehead. "I know she's a good girl, beta. My son wouldn't choose any ordinary girl. But please understand our problem too."

Maa was talking about completely contradictory things.

My parents and I started tearing up. Sometimes real love demands tears, sometimes everything; maybe it always demands sacrifices. How can a son accept that his most loving parents are crying because of him? I said, "Papa, Maa, don't cry for me. If you don't agree, it is okay, but please don't force me to sleep with any other girl," I said as I hugged my mother like a kangaroo kid and started cursing myself for being born in a Brahmin family.

My father continued to state the advantages of marrying within the same caste; like if I married a Brahmin girl I could become an IAS officer but not doing so would end in me being rejected from the post of a peon. But I remained in my mother's lap.

"Beta, if you want to, you can marry any other Brahmin girl. We're completely fine with it." His words burned me and I replied, "Papa, the day you find a better person, please let me know."

"Yes, there are a couple of proposals lined up for you. One of the girls is working in Pune at Infosys," he said like every female software professional was dying to marry me.

"Papa, this is the main problem," I said.

"What?"

"How will you find someone better than her? You don't even know her."

Operation Emotional Drama-1

I was at the Allahabad Railway station. The train was going to arrive in an hour. I called Bhavna. "Hi, Bhavna," I said in a low voice.

"I understand, Ajay. Please don't feel low." She had sensed my mood. "Please explain. Or should we talk tomorrow?"

"Bhavna, my family is not ready for this." I was about to start sobbing.

"Ajay, don't feel guilty. You're not responsible for anything," she said emotionally.

"We'll talk tomorrow. The train is about to arrive."

"Okay, happy journey dear, take care. Bye."

The Prayag Raj Express raced, as if desperate to kiss Delhi, my mind raced like a jet. Another storm started up in my mind.

I received an SMS from Bhavna after half an hour.

I know Ajay, it's difficult but don't get over burdened, will try to understand your parents.

Sometimes I don't understand what kind of girl she was. But she usually spoke from the heart. When someone speaks from the heart, it triggers the brain.

The positive side said: *A girl is ready to sacrifice a six-and-a-half year long loving relationship only because she doesn't want to hurt my parents; and on the other hand, my parents are against this marriage without even knowing her.* The negative side of mind had just one line to sing. *She is not a Brahmin. She is not a Brahmin.* I resolved: *I cannot leave her.*

We human being are like pigeons; if we are set free, we go back to our true homes. I concluded, *I want my parents and my love. I'm so lucky to be surrounded by three loving people and I cannot afford to lose any of them.*

The whole night, my cunning mind hatched a plan. I'd have to save myself from the tsunami. Next morning, I called my warrior.

"Hi, sweetheart. How are you?"

"Fine, dear," she said yawning.

"Listen, Bhavna. I love you and you're the best one for me."

"Pandeyji, so much confidence."

"Yes. If would-be Mrs Pandey is like you, then there is no chance of losing confidence."

"I would love to be called Mrs Pandey," she cheered.

"It's a commitment from the horse's mouth."

She giggled and said, "So what's the plan?"

"How did you know that I made a plan?" I asked, inquisitively.

"You can't leave me when I'm in trouble," she said emotionally. Sometimes she knew me even better than I knew myself. "So, what's the plan to transform Miss Bhavna Pradhan into Mrs Bhavna Pandey?" She giggled.

"Now, I'm going to fight in two different directions. My parents will try to resist until they become sure that we're inseparable."

"So?"

"So, I'm going to make a big emotional drama of not being well. I'll go for dieting kind of stuff and this will create a fear in their mind that I may commit suicide. And no parent wants that."

"But Ajay, how are you going to handle that? If something, happens to your family, then? I mean they are old. We should drop this idea," she said, concerned. Sometime, I feel she was more on my family's side.

"I'll keep an eye on them."

"But how? You're in Delhi and they are in Rihand Nagar."

She certainly asked every possible question.

"I have to talk to my local folk, my loving younger brother Monu."

"Are you sure Monu is going to help you... I mean us? What if he starts sneaking everything to your parents and what if he doesn't agree with you?"

"No chance, darling. I know my brother."

"Put me on a conference call while calling him. I'll be on mute and will listen to the conversation between the two great brothers."

"Okay."

"But..."

"I knew some 'but' would always be there in my story."

"But it's a time consuming process. It'll take months, may be a year?" she asked precisely. A beautiful mind always works well in love.

"I'm not done, dear. I'll go to Raipur to meet your parents."

"I doubt you can do that, Ajay. What will I say to them? You're going to Raipur for what?" she asked confused.

"No one will ask. I'm sure they'll be equally interested to meet their future son-in-law. Just tell them, the great Mr Pandeyji wants to meet them. Rest I'll handle," I boasted. "Hey, we should name our mission."

"Operation Blue Star," she suggested.

"We are not fighting against terrorists. How about Operation Emotional Drama?"

"Sounds good. Let's start with your drama, Pandeyji."

❖

On 1 January 2010, I started Operation Emotional Drama. I was on a conference call with Monu while Bhavna was on mute.

"Hello, younger brother. Wishing you a very happy new year."

"Same to you, *bhaiya*," Monu responded.

"Any news at home?"

"No. Mummy and Papa were sad," he responded.

"Listen carefully, Monu. You must be aware of Bhavna."

"Yes, I know Bhavna didi," he said innocently. I thought, *she could be your didi, not mine.*

"Brother, I revealed everything about Bhavna at home. Now maybe I'll start some emotional blackmail, but there is an equal chance that I'll get the same emotional drama from them as well. There are chances that this sentimental gun might backfire."

"I understand, bhaiya. So you want the updates," he said cleverly. He had never understood anything faster than this.

"Correct! So, please follow this plan. This drama may go on for months."

"Don't worry, bhaiya. Papa doesn't have any problem with Bhavna bhabhi. He is only worried about his brothers."

"What?" *What a confused guy? He started with Bhavna didi and has now jumped to Bhavna bhabhi. Bhavna probably could not have thought of a better end to this call.*

"Okay, brother. Focus on your studies as well, and make sure whenever you call, no one should be around," I wrapped up before he could attempt a new blunder.

"Okay, bye, bhaiya."

I hung up and called Bhavna again, thinking that she might think of Mr. Monu as a confused fellow.

"Hello Bhavna, did you listen?" I did not even complete my sentence, and Bhavna bhabhi interrupted.

"Your brother is really cute. I'm dying to be called bhabhi. Wow! He'll be the only one calling me bhabhi," she said cheerfully. "Imagine, Ajay. The both of us living together, making tiffin for you. When you go to office, I will kiss you and will say bye with added instructions to come soon. We'll share everyday office gossip too."

She was lost in her own daydreams. I felt relaxed and thanked god, *all beautiful girls are dumb.*

Delhi to Raipur

I t was the second week of January, 2010.

"Hi, darling. How are you?" Bhavna asked cheerfully over phone.

"Your excitement says you have some news."

"Yes, I'm excited because within the next two days you are going to meet my parents," she said. It was exciting for her but frightful for me.

"But I guess you have something else to tell me. What is the news?"

"Pooja didi wants to know what you like to eat," she said.

"That means I'm going to receive a grand welcome."

"Yes. The Pradhans are going to welcome the Pandeys," she said, proudly.

"Don't say 'Pandey' and 'Pradhan.' It scares me."

"Oh, that reminds me! You have to buy something for my family," she said.

"Am I going for a *muhdekhayi* rasam or what?" I yelled in frustration, "A return AC tatkal ticket from Delhi to Raipur costs more than four thousand bucks. I'm not going to invest anything more."

"Mr Kanjoos Pandeyji, you've to forget all these silly things. After all, you are going to marry a princess of the Pradhan family," She giggled. *Sometimes I hate her giggles.*

"Ms Princess, you're going to marry a beggar."

"The princess orders Mr Kanjoos to please make a list."

"List!" The word 'list' felt like a bomb.

"You've to buy one kilogram sweets from a branded shop like Nathu or Haldiram. No Agarwals."

"One kilo!" It sounded as if someone has asked a drunkard for his last peg.

"Your father is a diabetic. Pooja di must be on a diet. Mr Nanhu is only two years old. Your mummy will have one kilo of sweets or what?"

"You've to argue about everything. It's stupid to talk to you."

"You should get used to such things after we get married," she said giggling, and continued giving orders. "Now listen, Ajay. You've to buy a toy for Nanhu. It should be more than five hundred rupees, at least. I've to specify these things in your case," she said. She stressed the word 'least' as if it was just like donating a rupee to a beggar.

"He is a two-year-old kid, ma'am. Will he play with the toy or five hundred rupees? And does he even say anything?"

"He only says '*Angy*'. Sometime he says 'Mausi,' too," she said.

"Angy? Angelina Jolie?"

"No, Angy means, 'What is this?' It's a question for him," she explained.

"On one condition; if he calls me Mausaji. Tell Pooja di it's my wish to hear this from him," I said.

"Concentrate, Ajay."

And she continued giving a series of instructions.

"You have to make this journey memorable. You have to wear a blazer or coat. Please do shave on the train, and lastly, when they ask you to stay at home then you have to say no first. If they insist, only then you should accept," she instructed.

Hotel bills will also bomb on me. This journey would be memorable; my credit card will never allow me to forget it.

"What colour innerwear do I have to wear? Green or red?" I asked sarcastically. She chuckled. She gave me instructions again like a teacher. I followed them like those students who are all time busy cursing their teacher, but at the end of the day complete all homework with heavy hearts.

❖

The Indian railways had continued to follow their tradition; the Gondwana Express from Delhi to Raipur was delayed by six hours. I was in the train and preparing my thoughts for the upcoming meeting. I wasn't that tense as I'd already faced the worst at home. One question stumped me. I called my angel again.

"Hello, Bhavna."

"Are you in Raipur?"

"No, yaar, will reach in an hour."

"Listen Ajay, I want to tell you, you need not stay in a hotel," she giggled. "Now, happy? Hope you can save millions of dollars."

"Bhavna, the train charger is not working. Please listen carefully."

"Ok, go on."

"Should I call your mother and father 'Papa' and 'Mummy' or 'Uncle' and 'Aunty'?"

"Hmm," she thought for a second. "Uncle and Aunty would be nice."

"Okay, bye," I said

"One more thing. *Pair chhuu lena..*Touch their feet," she said and my phone went off.

❖

As soon as the train entered the Raipur railway station, I saw Bhavna's parents waiting outside the station and as my eyes moved along the platform, I saw a baby holding Pooja di's little finger.

Oh my god! Don't they have any other work to do? The whole family is here to receive me. Mr Pandey, you're the first person in your family who has come for his own muhdikhayi, your own marriage exhibition! I pretended I had not seen anyone and started looking at Mars and Jupiter. After two minutes, I heard a voice similar to Bhavna's.

"Ajay! Here, Ajay," Pooja di screamed.

I went to them and touched Bhavna's mummy's feet.

They gave her life. They deserve this, I thought.

"Namaste, Mum...Aunty."

"It's okay, beta," she said and caught my hand.

I smiled and was about to jump at Bhavna's papa's feet but he realized the upcoming danger and said, "It's completely okay."

The word 'completely' seemed as if touching his feet wasn't going to make much of a difference to him. I imagined a scene from *DDLJ* and thought. *Do I need to feed pigeons early in the morning to make an impact on Mr Amrish Puri?*

I took the front seat. There was silence inside the car. It was killing, but the silence was broken. "Angy?"

When there is a baby, silence does not last long. I heard the word, 'Angy', turned, and found a tiny little figure pointing at me. Mr Nanhu was enquiring about me.

"You want to come?" I pulled him into the front seat. He continued staring at me and said, "Angy."

"Mausaji," I said and Bhavna's father gave me a strange look. I grinned and heard Pooja di giggling at the back.

"Angy", the baby asked again. It felt as if he was saying, "Moron, you came here to take away my mausi."

"I'm uncle," I said, answering him.

I continued to play with him and was thankful for the presence of the kid in the car. He was the only one that kept us alive for the next half an hour. But I saw out of the corner of my eye that Bhavna's mummy was scanning me from head to toe. She must have counted every pimple, mole and strand of hair on my head. I was scared but I consoled myself. *Mr Pandey, your muhdikhayi has begun.*

After we reached Bhavna's house, with a heavy heart, I handed Bhavna's mummy one kilo of kaju sweets from Nathu Sweets and Nanhu a toy. He was delighted and tried to play with me, but my head was churning. After a thirty-six hour journey, everything exhausted me.

"Ajay, please have some tea and go and rest. You must be tired," Bhavna's mummy said, concerned. After a few minutes, many cups of tea, snacks, cashew nuts, namkeen, chips, sweets and cookies crowded the dining table.

Were they waiting for me or the whole baraat? If this is what it is like during a love marriage, they would have opened snack shops for an arranged marriage.

On seeing all the goodies on the table in front of me, I turned back into the monster I had been during my college days. I pounced on the salted cashews and the moment I thought I would finish them off, Bhavna's face flashed in front of me and I heard her saying, "Control, Pandeyji."

I took one with a fake grin as if it was the last cashew nut on this earth. I looked at Mummy and grinned.

"Take some more, beta," she said.

"It's okay, aunty."

After finishing a soothing cup of tea, I decided to summarize what I'd to say in a few minutes.

"I want some rest, aunty. My head is aching."

"Pooja," she called her daughter to guide me to the room.

After forty-five minutes of resting, Pooja di entered the room.

"Ajay, you want to talk to us before dinner or after dinner?"

I was thinking what to say when she made another suggestion.

"Ajay, it would be better to talk first, so that you can eat in peace," she smiled.

"Ok. I'm coming."

While leaving she said, "All the best, Ajay." Till then I was fine, but her 'all the best' froze me.

I entered the living room while praying to the hundreds of known gods.

They had already settled down on the sofa. Three pairs of eyes were staring at me; only one pair of eyes gave me some space. Nanhu was busy playing with the gadget I had gifted him. I gave them a fake smile and settled on the sofa.

"Nanhu, please don't make any noise. Settle down," Bhavna's mummy seemed to be preparing herself for the upcoming primetime show.

Mr Nanhu also joined them and now four pairs of eyes were staring at me. My throat felt choked. In spite of such a big living area, I felt as if we were all packed inside a toilet. My mobile blinked as I received a message.

Love you, Ajay. I know Mr Shahrukh will rock. Muaah.

There was no doubt; that message had helped me breathe. After reading the SMS, I turned towards Bhavna's father to say what I had practised.

"Uncle, you know why I am here. I've known Bhavna for almost seven years and we studied together in engineering. Yes, we are good friends. After engineering, I decided to do an MBA and now I'm placed in Redington India Limited, in Delhi," I spluttered. "My papa is an engineer at NTPC, Rihand Nagar; I have three siblings."

I was talking like I was being interviewed for a job. Then I pushed myself. *Ajay, please don't go round and round in circles. Please come straight to the point.* I gulped down a glass of water and continued.

"All my paternal relatives live in Naini, Allahabad. My father is the youngest in the family and we live in a joint family. Being the youngest brother, he has to consult each and every family member. An inter-caste marriage is still taboo among Brahmins," I sighed. "But I know my father loves me and he'll respect my decision." I tried to generalize my problem to get the specific solution.

"Bhavna already explained that," Bhavna's mummy interrupted me.

"Mummy, I want two favours from Papa," I said 'Mummy' so that they would consider me as a part of the family.

"Yes, please tell me, beta," Bhavna's Papa said.

"Because my father requires some time to convince his brothers, I need some time from you and..." I paused for a minute and continued, "Secondly, my family feels a sense of pride in belonging to the groom's side. Tomorrow they may expect the first call from you."

"That's all?" His voice echoed like that of the legendary Amrish Puri in my mind.

"One more. Last one," I already said two and now I had to add the third.

"I may be portraying an unpractical scenario; tomorrow my father would ask you to convince Bhavna against this marriage. So I need your support in that."

"It means your father is totally against this," he hit the nail straight on the head.

"No, uncle. Personally, papa doesn't have any issue, but the other relatives or tauji may disagree," I lied.

"Your family knows about this?"

"Yes, my family knows about Bhavna."

"No, I'm not talking about Bhavna. Your trip to Raipur."

"No this is an unofficial trip. And you must keep it a secret," I said as if I was applying for an unofficial visa.

"Your fourth favour," he summed up and I nodded.

I froze. Everyone was glaring at me. In fact, Mr Nanhu was also looking at me in a way as if saying, 'You can't snatch away my Mausi.' I excused myself to go to the washroom. I thanked god for creating the biological need to urinate. I intentionally took a lot of time and tried to hear what was going on from the other side of the door, but failed. To break the silence, I came out with a fake smile and tried to dangle another carrot in front of them.

"Uncle, My father is a loving person. He only wants to see me happy. He will not expect a dowr ..."

But my words were cut off by him.

"Listen, son. We belong to a simple family and we don't have any problem with this. I want my daughter to be happy. You take your time and even if I'd decided on an arranged marriage, I would have definitely been the first caller. So, calling your parents is not a big problem. Just tell me what is the best time to talk to them, but..." I have always hated the word 'but...' he continued. "I've only one condition – this marriage should be an arranged marriage. I'll not support it if your family does not agree to it."

"What if my father calls you to warn you against this marriage?" My proposal was like anticipatory bail for Bhavna.

"You don't worry, son. Take your time to convince your family."

Tears filled my eyes. My heart said, *This man is not Amrish Puri; he is like Anupam Kher of DDLJ who always seeks happiness in the happiness of his son.*

"You don't worry about time, beta. But the sooner will be better."

This time Bhavna's mother interrupted us.

I realized one thing. I only had limited time to convince my family. The more I delayed the process, the higher the chances of her mother turning from Farida Jalal to Lalita Pawar.

We got up for dinner and as expected, a five star buffet was served. Bhindi ki sabzi, daal tadka, roti, and dum aloo. I understood who might have told them to make all this. Now, I felt like the prince of the family. I stuffed myself with food and ignored any thought of "Control Pandeyji".

❖

The next morning, I was served a lavish breakfast. I was ready to leave to catch the Sampark Kranti which left at noon. I touched Bhavna's mummy's feet. Pooja di wished me: "Happy journey, Ajay." Bhavna's papa was taking out the car when I heard a cute melodious voice: "Mausaji".

I turned to the source. Mr Nanhu was pointing his tiny finger at me. I looked at Pooja di and she winked. I pulled him up on my lap, kissed his cheeks and whispered into his ear.

"Your mausi is awesome and it's a commitment that one day I'll officially be your mausaji."

But again, he said innocently, "Angy".

Operation Emotional Drama - 2

My emotional drama was at its pinnacle. Silence had become my language with my parents. I didn't miss any opportunity to let them know that I was heartbroken. Monu updated me with the progress everyday which was not really any progress at all. I decided to ignore Papa's calls, but the son's heart sometimes disobeyed the resolve and picked the call. Papa noted down my roommates' mobile numbers and whenever I didn't pick his call, he called my roommates to check if everything was fine. My heart was burdened with guilt and I cursed myself for emotionally blackmailing them. I was feeling down. My conscience often shouted "You are a bad son... You are a bad son."

"How can you be a bad son when you feel guilty about every lie? Your guilty conscience says that you are a good son," Bhavna consoled me. In spite of my illogical act, Bhavna always found some logical reason to cheer me up.

Though I was the one who had launched Operation Emotional Drama, both sides were playing well. One day, my mother was hospitalized and was discharged on the same day.

"Due to excessive thinking, she had a mild pain near the heart and the doctor said there is a chance of heart trouble," Papa explained like I was solely responsible for her condition. Monu was not at home, as he was busy with his entrance exams. The next day when he was back, I called him. But he refused to talk as he was with Maa at the hospital. The situation was getting worse. I was scared and called Bhavna.

"Hi, dear. How are you?" she asked.

"It was rubbish; Maa had to go to the hospital again."

"What? Has she been hospitalized again?" Bhavna asked, shocked.

"I don't know whether she has been hospitalized or not. I called Monu. He said that he is in the hospital with Maa."

"Oh Ajay, I think you should go home. This emotional drama had been going on for the last two months. Go to your home before it is too late." Her concern, love, and sensitivity to people was what I loved the most about her.

"Love you, dear. You are always concerned about...Oh, Monu is calling."

"I want to listen to this conversation, Ajay. I'll remain on mute during the conference call," she pleaded.

"No Bhavna. I don't want you to hear any bad news."

"Ajay, I'm also concerned. Tomorrow they could be my family."

Again her saint behaviour made me faint.

I called Monu; Bhavna stayed on the line.

"Hi brother, how is Maa?"

"Namaste, bhaiya. Maa is fine. How are you?"

"I'm fine."

"Are you sure you are fine?" Monu asked, inquisitively.

"Still alive, brother. Only worried about Maa and Papa's health."

"Good to hear that. Papa asked me about your health. They are worried about you and you are worried about them," Monu replied.

"What did you say about me?"

"Nothing. I said, 'bhaiya is not talking much'. That's all."

"How is Maa? Is she okay? What did the ECG report say?"

"The ECG report is normal," Monu said.

"Then, why was she hospitalized yesterday?"

"Brother, wait! Maa was not hospitalized because of heart trouble. She was hospitalized because of a gas problem."

Suddenly a voice chuckled in the background.

"Bhaiya, is someone on a conference call?" Monu asked.

"No no, it was a sound from the TV. I just turned it on."

I mentally cursed Bhavna for not keeping her phone on mute.

"Forget that sound. So you mean Maa is okay? No heart trouble?"

"No Bhaiya. It's all emotional drama, but they are sad about you."

"Listen carefully, bro. In case there is any such danger, you'll have to handle it and inform me. Do you understand?"

"Don't worry, bhaiya. You take care of yourself."

"I'm fine as long as they are okay, dear."

"Bhaiya, I have to go else Papa will guess that I was talking to you, then he'll start using me."

"Using? What does that mean? Am I using you?"

"Oh, no, bhaiya. I love being used by you since you are going to give me such a lovely bhabhi." His words touched me.

"How do you know that your bhabhi is lovely?"

"Bhaiya, you ask so many questions. I'm going now. Bye."

"Bye."

And Monu said, "And bye, bhabhi."

"Thank you, Monu," Bhavna said.

"What is this? Now I understood why you said your bhabhi was lovely. You were buttering her up."

I heard a beep from the other end of the line.

Now Bhavna and I were on the line.

"Ma'am, can't you keep your cell phone on mute?"

"Sorry, but your brother is a big fan of mine," Bhavna said flattered. "He is really cute."

"He is not cute. He is my bother, after all. He realized that you were on call too and he said the same to butter you up."

"So, your entire family is like that?" she asked.

"Yes, my father is turning my mother's gas problem into a heart problem."

"Your entire family is involved in Operation Emotional Drama." She chuckled.

"It's not the time to analyze the smartness of my family."

"Mr Pandey, just answer one thing: while proposing to me, were you not aware of all these issues?" she asked bitterly.

"Love is blind dear." I sighed

"But lovers are dumb."

My quilt and my guilt

Operation Emotional Drama had been running unsuccessfully for over three months and how long it would last could not be guessed. Every day, I projected my sadness as a warm heat so that the candle could melt and I could give that liquid my darling's shape.

1 February 2010 was my father's fiftieth birthday. A good day for celebration, but if someone had a son like me, then every day could have a reason to mourn. And besides, my birthday gift was also going to call him from Raipur. It was decided that on my father's birthday, Bhavna's dad would talk to my father.

I was waiting for Bhavna's call. I was eager to receive the feedback of the conversation between both the fathers. Bhavna called me. I disconnected and called her back.

"Ajay, I love you, yaar."

She said the world's loveliest lines while sobbing in a way that horrified me.

"Love you, too, my darling. But what happened? First stop crying and then explain."

She continued sobbing.

"Bhavna, please tell me what's wrong, dear!"

"Papa called your father. First, he wished him a happy birthday and later when Papa started talking about our marriage, he said..." She broke down and started weeping.

"No need to say anything, darling. He must have said that you convince Bhavna and I'll handle my son, since my other family members will not agree to an inter-caste marriage."

"Yes, you are so intelligent," she said recovering.

"Was Papa rude?"

"No, your father was pretty gentle and soft spoken."

"What did your father say? That's more important."

"He said both are young, earning and mature; we should understand them. We're young kids and can be swayed in any direction. Still, he left the decision to your father; he said, 'After all he is your son and you have every right to make his decisions'."

"Oh! Such a lovely father."

"Yes, Ajay. I never expected this from my strict father. Today, I forgive him for everything. If I was at Raipur, I would have hugged him," she said in a choked voice.

"Parents are like that, only. So don't worry if your father behaves like that. Surely my father will also melt someday."

"I love you, Ajay. My father didn't do this for me. He supported you against your father only because of your visit to Raipur."

"I knew this would happen. That's why I was proactive about going to Raipur."

"But, Ajay. There is one serious problem," she sighed.

"What now? Tell me."

"If next time your papa requests the same from him, then my father will also say no. Now, both have each other's numbers as well."

"I can understand yaar. Even I'm scared about that," I said, tensed.

"Ajay, now you've less time to convince your parents," she said as if I had millions of years to negotiate with them before this.

"I knew this scene; but I've a pla...."

"Another plan!" She interrupted me. "Why don't you join the Planning Commission, even they plan less than you," she cried. "Your Operation Emotional Drama was crap; I don't want to be part of any plan now."

"Listen, yaar..." But she was in no mood to listen.

"If you're so intelligent and you know everything, then why did you propose to me? Your family has so many issues. Why did you come into my life? I was happy alone," she said furious. I remained quiet. She kept on asking me, "Why, Ajay? Why?"

"Sorry, Bhavna. I don't have answers to your questions."

"I'm a simple girl, Ajay. I don't want money or a high profile life. I only want my family to be happy. I owe them for the way they are supporting me. If tomorrow we get married and have kids, I'll not add any surname to their name. I hate this Pandey and Pradhan. I'll kill the bastards who made this caste system. We're born human beings and should be loved for our actions. I fail to understand Ajay, how someone is responsible for their birth?" She cried.

I was about to say something but the call got disconnected. I called back, but her phone was switched off. I buried myself under the quilt and started cursing my fortune. I begged the gods who I used to only think of occasionally, but had now begun to think of more frequently. I tried to reach Bhavna multiple times, but failed.

At around 1.00 a.m., I received a message from Bhavna.

Sorry for shouting at you, Ajay. You are facing more than I am, and I really respect you for standing up for the right reasons. I love your 'never give up' attitude to life. I'm okay. Will talk tomorrow.

❖

The situation, however, didn't improve and negativity started taking over. We started talking less and Bhavna started avoiding interview calls from Delhi too. I stopped giving her daily updates about my family.

Why did I involve Bhavna in all this? Why was I born a Brahmin? In fact, why was I born? Why did I have to struggle all the time? Should I have continued with this? Suppose they agreed to the match with her, how would she adjust to them? Was I a bad person? I asked myself questions but they remained unanswered every time.

The positive side of my mind stopped arguing with the negative. I felt like hugging my mother and crying. Hopelessness and helplessness alone were part of my daily breakfast. I even stopped eating breakfast.

One weekend, I bought a few Breezers in order to dissolve into that. A breezer can do wonders for a person who never drinks. I opened my laptop to find a health tip from my company.

Mental health

According to studies, one out of every four Indians suffers from an anxiety disorder. If not addressed in time, anxiety may lead to serious depression. Mental or emotional health refers not only to the absence of anxiety or depression, but your overall psychological well being. It includes the way you feel about yourself, the quality of your relationships and your ability to manage your feelings and deal with difficulties.

Red flag feelings and behaviour that may require help:

1. *Inability to sleep.*
2. *Concentration problems that affect your professional or personal life.*
3. *Using nicotine, food, drugs or alcohol in order to cope with difficult emotions.*

4. Negative or self-destructive thoughts.
5. Thoughts of death and suicide.

Issued by World Federation for Mental Health and World Health Organisation.

I read this after drinking two whole breezers and wondered, *How is WHO aware of my problems? Who let them know? Every four Indians are suffering from this? Even Brahmins? Aren't they excluded on account of the good deeds from their previous births? Who keeps an account of the deeds of all our previous births?*

And with those thoughts, Operation Emotional Drama died a quick death.

As I was reading about the red flags, I received a call from Monu.

"Hi, bhaiya. How are you and how is bhabhi?"

"I'm fine as usual. Don't call her 'bhabhi'. She is not on a conference call with us."

"But she is still my bhabhi."

"Stop eating my head about your bhabhi," I shouted. "Sorry, yaar," I apologized recovering from my own agony.

"I can understand, bhaiya. I have news."

"Good or bad?"

"That you have to decide."

"A new serial started on TV a few days back. It shows on Colors at 9.00 p.m. and Papa and Maa watch it a lot."

"What is so special about it? Has someone committed suicide in it, or what?"

"Just watch it, you'll see."

I put on Colors and for the first time, I watched something seriously. It started with some stereotypical music and the trailer during the breaks said, *'Brahmin ka ladka aur kayasth ki ladki.'*

The effect of the breezer vanished after I saw that. The serial was called *Ye Pyaar Na Hoga Kam*. It was the love story set in a small town in Lucknow. The boy belonged to rich Brahmin family and the girl belonged to poor Kayastha family. It starred Yami Gautam and Gaurav Khanna. The serial added salt to my wounds.

I yelled at myself. "What is this? Is some serial going to decide my fate or what?"

I seriously followed a serial for the first time in my life. And in fact, Bhavna's family was also following the same serial. It showed all the problems and differences between two castes. One was pure vegetarian and the other one was non-vegetarian. The Kayastha family was miserly whereas the Brahmins were rich and affluent. The Kayasthas were good at business whereas the Brahmins were quite simple. Bhavna did not have a TV at her PG, so she couldn't watch it. I'm still thankful to her landlord for not having a TV.

I started hating everything: my job, my family, my friends and even myself. Even the work in the office was not keeping me occupied. I often used to give fake reasons and would stay buried inside my quilt. Those days my quilt was my best friend. Every time when I was buried inside my quilt, my guilt was above that.

Love you, everyone

After a few days, I received a call from my friend. This news really depressed me. I don't know whether I should mention that news in this book or not. But I cannot avoid that...so sorry buddy.

The girlfriend of one of my best friends in my MBA program had committed suicide due to depression. I informed Papa about it and decided to go to Mumbai. I hunted for tickets on the IRCTC website, but getting a train ticket immediately was almost as tough as getting to the KBC hot seat. And, of course, I wasn't lucky enough. So, I booked tickets for Holi.

I called Bhavna. "Hi, Bhavna, I have some bad news."

"Tell me something new, Ajay. Go on I'm ..."

"Bhavna, it's not about my family. You remember Vaibhav?"

"Yes, your MBA best buddy."

"Ya. Remember, I talked about his girlfriend?"

"Yes, they were going to get married."

"She committed suicide."

"What?" She said shocked. After a few seconds, she asked, "But why?"

"Don't know. But I'm planning to go to Mumbai during Holi."

After a pause of two seconds she said, "Will call you, Ajay."

Her voice was low and I'm sure she was about to cry. She called back after fifteen minutes.

"Sorry, Ajay," she said in a very low voice.

"Don't hide you tears. We can't help it, yaar."

It's a unique human behaviour that when you tell someone not to cry, they will cry more.

"Ajay, I'm not crying for Vaibhav, I'm crying for you."

"I'm fine, darling," I said.

"Sorry, Ajay. You never leave a person when he is in trouble. Look, you are going to Mumbai to meet your friend. On the contrary, I'm putting unnecessary pressure on you. Ajay, I'll marry only you... even if it takes a million years. No need to worry about anything; I'll manage."

Her words made me tear up.

"It is so nice of you to say that dear, but don't cry like this. Even I'm not going to leave you," I said, hiding my tears.

She cried even louder and said, "Ajay, promise me you'll never commit suicide in your life, no matter how difficult the situation might be."

"Why would I commit suicide? I've a beautiful person like you to share my life with."

"Whether I'm with you or not, if you lose interest in life, start living for others."

"I'll never commit suicide darling. I'm not a coward. Remember what we say?"

"Yes, you'll never surrender."

❖

The next day, Monu called me.

"Hi bhaiya. I've news."

"Good or bad?"

"That you have to decide," he said impishly.

"Okay, go on, I'm up for anything."

"Bhaiya, listen carefully. Mummy and Papa are ready to accept bhabhi."

"They are ready?" I said in disbelief. I had not been ready for this.

"Papa informed Mummy about Vaibhav's situation and she knows about Vaibhav, too."

"Yes, she met him once in Pune."

"Maa and Papa think that if they don't agree to the match between you and bhabhi, you might also commit suicide. So, Maa exploded at Papa saying, 'I want only my son, I don't know anything about Brahmin or Kayastha.'"

Suddenly, I received a call from Maa.

"Monu, Maa is calling me. Will talk to you later."

I called my mother back

"Hi, Maa."

"How is Bhavna?"

"Which Bhavna, the Kayastha one?" I said bitterly.

"No, my bahu Bhavna," she said and my eyes started getting wet.

"Bahu? What a change, Maa? How did this miracle happen?"

"I don't know. I only want my son to be happy," she said. Her words caused a lump in my throat.

"Love you, Maa."

"Love you too, my son," she said. But the other side of her character again pulled her towards the Kayastha pole. "I know she is completely vegetarian but..."

"Stop watching serials, Maa." I knew where this was coming from.

"Stop arguing with me. You cowardly young generation, running to commit suicide."

"Why don't you talk to her directly?"

"Yes, put her on a conference call."

I dialled Bhavna, by keeping Maa on hold, "Listen, Bhavna, you are on a conference call with Maa. She is ready to accept you as her bahu and wishes to talk to you. So, are you ready?"

"I'm ready for everything," she said.

"Listen, you have to say Maa, not Aunty, okay?" I instructed.

Now, I was part of a scary conference call: a mother, a would be daughter-in-law and a son. Some scenes from a typical saas-bahu serial flashed in my mind.

"Namaste, Maa," Bhavna said.

"How are you, Bhavna?"

"Fine, Maa, how are you?" Bhavna said.

"I'm good, beta. Sorry Bhavna, we are not against you at all. I believe in my son, but you know we were bound by our societies. Even being born as a Brahmin, he hardly believes in god. I totally believe in god and my heart says I'm doing the right thing. I hope you too believe in him."

Whenever my mother gets emotional, she talks senseless things. I thought I should interrupt her before she starts asking her about scriptures and sermons.

"She strongly believes in god, Maa, even more than you do."

"You don't interrupt in the middle when we're talking."

I realized a son should never interrupt when a saas and bahu's discussion is going on.

Maa and Bhavna talked for a while and the call ended. It brought great relief, finally. Now my father was fighting alone like Ashwasthama, the last warrior of the *Mahabharata*. But the cunning Arjuna inside me said that Operation Emotional Drama would win.

The same night, I got a call from my father. He talked emotionally,

"Sonu, caste and religion is important because we live in a world where you are alone if you do not belong to one. I understand the world is changing and I wish that one day we could think beyond this man-made discrimination of caste and religion. Until then, we have to deal with the society. We are social animals; perhaps more animal than social."

I remained silent and listened to him intently.

"My dear son, you are my flesh and blood, and nothing is more important to me than you. You are my world. When a child is born, he brings a lot of hope and joy for the parents. When one does something stupid, it's just a moment of pain for them, but lifelong misery for their loved ones. I wonder why they don't understand the pain of the ones for whom they are the only purpose in life. I don't know why..." He was silent for a few seconds. I understood that he was trying not to cry.

"Look Sonu, if you believe that you will be happy with Bhavna, you have our blessings. I know you both will make a happy couple."

He sighed, "Remember Sonu, you are my brave son." I couldn't see his tears, but sensed the trembling in his voice. I don't understand why a father always puts up a tough face; but my father proved that they are not that tough after all.

After two minutes, we disconnected the call.

I texted him, *I love you, and, you are the best father*

I felt as though something was stuck in my throat, choking me. I ran to the washroom and opened the tap, so that the sounds of my sobbing were drowned by the sound of the water. My heart was overburdened with guilt and my lips started quivering. I sat on the commode and cried in earnest. No crocodile tears, no Operation Emotional Drama.

I said to myself, "You're a bad son. You're surrounded by loving parents, who only care for you. Thank you, God, for giving me such a lovely mother, father, brother and such a loving partner." I continued crying and said, "Love you, Monu. Love you, Papa. Love you, Maa. Love you, Bhavna. Love you, everyone."

My happiest video clip

After seven years of friendship, love, struggle, drama and emotions, the 4th of July was the date finalized for the Brahmin ladka to marry the Kayastha ladki. Of course, we were happy. It was a dream come true, and our happiness doubled at the news of her job offer in Noida at CSC India Ltd.

The fourth of July, 2010 was the only day I felt like I was really special. All eyes were on me. It was making me even more nervous than my first audition performance at IERT. My father was downhearted since the other relatives had refused to come. On the contrary, the bride was so happy that her face went completely round and her dimples vanished under the heavy makeup.

Finally, the much awaited *jaimaal* ceremony or garland exchange took place and Bhavna's relatives and my friends took over the dance floor. We watched them dance. I remained calm, serious and silent by hiding my nervousness behind my fictitious grin. All the other relatives were busy desperately hogging the food. Bhavna was blushing beside me. She was shining as bright as a bulb that could burst with happiness any time. I felt a small vibration on the stage because the stage was made of plywood; it would vibrate even if a kid walked across it.

I had failed after serious attempts to find the source of the vibration. I looked around the stage but apart from bride and groom, no one was there. Then I realized that the bride was the source. She was tapping her feet to the music. It had gone unnoticed because she was wearing a sari.

"Ma'am, what happened?" I whispered to her, while looking in Mars and Jupiter direction.

"I feel like dancing, Ajay," she mumbled.

"Control, Bhavna. Papa is watching, see. He would not like his daughter-in-law dancing with so many eyes on her."

Asking Bhavna not to dance was like asking a government officer not to take bribe.

"Ajay, a wedding happens once; we'll not get married again."

"Control, Bhavna, please."

Before our marriage, Bhavna used to say 'control'; now I was pleading for the same. Marriage does make us change.

"Do it, Ajay. Do it for your wife. You'll remember this forever," she pleaded and her whispered words touched me. My heart said, *Anything for my wife.*

I called one friend and whispered, "*Saale kamine*, dancing alone."

"You also come."

"Listen to my plan." This time I laughed at myself when I said the word 'plan' and Bhavna glared at me like I'd committed a cardinal sin.

"Listen carefully; you have to come here after five minutes with Pooja di and force us to dance. Remember, I'll keep saying no, but you have to insist till we agree."

After five minutes, he came to us and pretended to force me to dance. After half a dozen heartless rejections, finally, I jumped on the dance floor and thought I should call the bride as well. I turned around for her, but she was already standing on the dance floor. We danced uncontrollably for the next five minutes. My father kept glaring at us like the legendary Amrish Puri in *DDLJ* but we remained lost in Mars and Jupiter.

She had given me the happiest video clip of my life.

❖

Hopefully, she was the rare Indian bride who'd leave her family with a smile on her face. It doesn't mean that she was not sad about leaving her mother. She made a deliberate attempt not to say bye to anyone with tears. She hugged me inside the hotel room and broke down like a weak lady. I hugged her in a fatherly way and tried to pacify her. She went on asking me, "Why do girls have to go to the boys' homes? Why do only women have to bear all this pain in life? And more specifically, why me? Why can't we live with them? Why, Ajay?"

I didn't answer. Each time, I just managed to respond, "It will be fine, baby."

That day has given me an opportunity to understand why we usually call our girlfriends 'baby'. There is a father in every man and a child in every girl.

The quality of life is
what matters

After our wedding, we had chosen Kashmir for our honeymoon. The valley of love would soon be populated with two more official lovers. Yes, marriage is the license for love in India. Bhavna was full of joy. We were excited. It's always soothing to see one's loved one happy like that.

The three of us were roaming around on a shikara in Dal Lake. The third one was the boatman. The boat's seats had a dark red background printed with flowers. The view of the water all round us along with the snowy hills, the chirping birds and my princess in my arms made it a beautiful moment. Comfortable cushions covered in red velvet made us feel like we were lying on a bed covered in rose petals. I felt like a king cruising with his queen. I wrapped my left arm around her and she comfortably adjusted herself to my embrace. The view of the lake was mesmerizing. The water was perfectly calm, but our voices constantly interrupted the silence of the lake. We were brimming with romance.

"Ajay, why did you insist that we go for a honeymoon? We could have postponed this trip. Enough money has been spent during our wedding."

"Darling, there is a time to celebrate everything. Remember, a honeymoon delayed, is a honeymoon denied.'

"Pandeyji *ke fundey aur logic!*" She frowned. "But look, Ajay, sailing on Dal Lake is really romantic. See my mehandi is looking nice, no? It's still visible, just smell it." She covered my nose with her palms, so I couldn't smell anything else. That's the problem when you marry. You have to praise everything all the time.

"Wow! It's awesome," I said, but she looked doubtful. But being a woman, she liked what I said.

"Ajay, we struggled and did so much drama for our marriage, isn't it like *Amar Prem Kahani* types?"

"I hate *Amar Prem Kahani, Laila Majnu, Heer Ranjha* type of stories. None of them were practical people. I hate their suicidal endings."

"So rude! Not expected," she said shocked. "Who had a love marriage a few days ago?"

"Ma'am, someone has to die in an *amar prem kahani.*"

She gave me a confused look.

"See Bhavna, the famous love stories, movies and legends, which are immortal in the subjects of love, they failed in the biggest subject of respecting and living their own lives."

"I never thought of that," she said quietly. Even a chatterbox shuts her mouth when her mind is at work.

"So, Ajay, does it mean all the lovers in these legends are losers?"

"Yes, there is no such thing as an Amar Prem Kahani in real life."

"No, Ajay. I have a different opinion here," she said like rejecting my plea in court.

"Hmm," I said feeling like my objection was overruled.

"All these lovers are not known for their failures in life, but the quality of life they lived," she explained.

"Quality?"

This went over my head.

"Yes, Ajay, life is a journey. Every person who is born will die someday. Some celebrate a silver jubilee, some golden and some score a century, but life is not evaluated on the basis of number of the years spent on this earth," she said. It felt like I was sitting in front of a *guru mata*. I frowned, but didn't say anything, since I was getting a valuable life lesson for the first time, that too from my wife.

She continued, "The quality of life is what matters, not the quantity."

"Can you elaborate?" I said, behaving dumb.

"Now, rewind your life, Ajay, and think about the best incidents you can remember."

I started remembering, "Hmm...when I was appointed the captain of the school, hmm...When I scored the golden goal in a football match, when you accepted my love...hmm..."

"Pandeyji, bad at remembering the best things in your life," she interrupted.

"You tell," I said to avoid any further embarrassment.

She started in euphoric tone. "Hmm...when my tenth and twelfth results came out," I sighed; this haunted me.

"Dancing with you in the rain on our Pune trip, anchoring for you, holding my sister's baby Nanhu for the first time, when he called me 'mausi' for the first time, dancing with Pooja di at home, your surprise gifts, your placement news, engagement announcement, my CSC offer letter for Noida, bridal makeup, photo shoot for our marriage."

"Hold, hold, ma'am...let's come back to the point. I'm jealous... such a long list."

"Think of a twenty-five-year-old person, who had a hundred such experiences and a fifty year old person who has had seventy-five such experiences. So, who is meaner towards the life?"

"The younger one, of course," I said, stunned.

"Correct, Pandeyji, the quality of life is what matters, not the quantity." I was mute and didn't say anything. This time, I was the one using my brain and suddenly, Bhavna flicked a few drops of lake water at my face.

"Ajay, my first shikara ride is going to be added to the list," she chuckled.

"So, you like those stories about suicidal lovers?" I asked, inquisitively.

"Never. There are many people who are fighting every day to live life with their loved ones, and these over-emotional fools killed themselves. I don't respect them at all."

"But, Bhavna, every day is special for someone who is in love. One can remember it throughout their life."

"Correct, that's why every love story is unique."

"Yes, but we are super unique."

"Why?"

"Who discusses all these things on their honeymoon?"

"This is a lesson in romantic theory."

"A honeymoon is not for theory; let's start some practicals," she laughed.

A house turns into a home

After our wedding, we shifted to Noida. There were certain things in my life that had doubled after marriage. I had two of everything. Double packages, double the family members, double rooms, a double bed, double the set of parents and double the reasons to come home early. In short, my happiness was doubled. Bhavna's date to join CSC was delayed by a week. This gave us an additional week's holiday to turn our house into a home.

But I had to resume work at my office in Okhla, Delhi. On Monday morning at around seven, my sleep was disturbed by the sound of loud music. I thought Bhavna was listening to it, but when I opened my eyes heavy with sleep, she was not around. I heard the sound of utensils in the kitchen. I yawned and with my eyes half open, I walked towards the kitchen. To my surprise, I found a figure, dancing and swaying, playing with a kadhai.

After a few seconds of watching this dance in confusion, I realized who it was.

Oh, it's my wife!

My eyes were now wide open in happiness. It is always enjoyable to see your beloved dancing like this. I didn't disturb her and kept watching her moves. After two minutes, she turned around.

"Good morning, Pandeyji."

"Good morning, darling."

She lowered the flame, held my hands and started swaying gracefully to the rhythmic beats playing on TV.

"Dance, Ajay!"

At first, I refused the invitation, but gave in to her enthusiasm and started dancing along with her. Yes, after marriage every husband has to dance. I started singing and dancing to the song, *Billo Rani, kaho to abhi jaan de doon.* But my steps made her burst out into laughter.

"Ajay, your steps are unique!"

"Unique! Yes, Pandeyji style!" I said, proudly.

"Where did you learn all those steps? In your hostel?"

"It's a unique dance style. All the hostellers called them 'Pandey's steps'."

"Oh, any new steps you learned during your MBA?" I did the same steps again and she burst out laughing.

"Where did you perform these steps?"

"During the Ganpati Viserjan processions, for Lord Ganesha's farewell in Pune."

She smiled, came close to me and whispered, "I feel like I'm dancing with some roadside loafer."

"Go to hell!" I joked. "I won't dance."

"Pandeyji, but I love you," she said and hugged me.

"How can you love a loafer? And that too a roadside loafer?"

"No, I love a person who dances for me even without knowing the steps." I passed a smile. Her explanation touched me, I never noticed life the way she did. I went to the washroom and thought, *What a good way to start a day. Thanks Bhavna, for adding one more sweet memory to my life.*

After an hour, when I was about to leave for office, she said,

"Ajay, your tiffin box for lunch."

I smiled. For the first time, I was carrying a tiffin box to office. *Welcome to married life, Pandeyji!*

"Please hold the box like Shahrukh Khan did in *Rab Ne Bana Di Jodi*," she said as she hugged me.

I adjusted my helmet and as I was about to start the bike, I looked up towards the balcony. My wife blew me a flying kiss and I pretended to catch it like nectar had fallen from the sky, a single drop of which could convert the entire Noida locality into a glorious Kumbh Mela. This continued every day, week after week. We started loving our weekends for new reasons. I had more time to sleep and she had more time to cook and dance.

❖

We were not a girl and a boy anymore; we were now becoming a mature and loving couple. Bhavna was the owner of the kitchen. I always said, the kitchen belongs to you and being an owner of the kitchen, you've the full right to the place. But that was the cardinal sin I did.

She changed the kitchen completely. She parcelled off my old utensils and got new ones. The kitchen was not the only room to be turned around. She had got a new sofa, showpieces and a dressing table. She turned my messy house into a presentable home. Every weekend she would shop for utensils, curtains and other knick-knacks while I would bargain with the salespersons.

Now, I had two sets of parents. My phone bill also doubled but calls between Reliance numbers were free and that was the saving grace. My family always helped during a crisis, but they also left me alone during the happy days.

Papa, Maa and Monu – all three of them started talking to Bhavna. I hardly received any calls from any of them. Even more ironic was the fact that though I was the subject of their conversations, I seemed to be second on everyone's priority lists. It didn't feel bad, though. I loved the way Bhavna accepted my family. It'd been about one month since we had been married. I was enjoying the small changes that marriage brings. But not all of them were enjoyable.

A month after being married, Bhavna normally left office after I did, and usually came home after I did. I reached home and was surprised that she was already home and was wearing a sari.

"Wow! You look awesome. What happened? How are you home early?"

"You forgot the date."

"Is today something special?" I asked puzzled.

"Hmm...Today is fourth August."

"Is it your birthday or something?" I asked, scared.

"This means you don't remember my birthday!" She glared.

I joked, "I do but..."

"Leave it, just come inside."

She cut me short.

In the living room, I found a bouquet of flowers and a black forest cake, with a lit candle on it. *Is today my birthday?*

I went up to the candle and started guessing.

"Is it the day you joined Satyam? Or maybe, Pooja di's birthday? Monu's birthday?"

I failed and after a number of guesses, I finally decided to ask her directly.

"What is the occasion, darling?" I grinned, innocently.

"Our one month marriage anniversary."

"What!" I was confused and did not know whether to be happy or sad. To keep her spirits up, I said, "Congratulations, Bhavna."

"Same to you, darling."

"Okay, let's capture the moment." I took some pictures with a fake smile still on my face. I was physically present, but my worried mind was somewhere else.

"Bhavna, I have a question. I hope you will not mind."

"Go on," she said, with her mouth full of cake.

"So, are we going to have this 'anniversary' the fourth of every month?" I grinned, fearfully.

"Are you scared thinking about having to get a cake and a bouquet every month, and spending your precious money?" She laughed madly.

"Not exactly," I said touching her. "I'm asking because I want to know if every month I will get to see you in a sari." I cleverly changed the subject.

"I can wear a sari every day, Ajay, if you like. Don't you worry. I only did all this because it's our first month anniversary."

"You are always welcome, ma'am." I heaved a sigh of relief.

"You are a kanjoos pandit," she giggled.

"Okay listen, this Saturday a few of my friends will come for lunch," I said, trying to change the subject.

"Why didn't you ask me?"

"What is there to ask? I'm calling my friends..." I shrugged.

"It's just that... I've not bought any serving utensils."

"What have we been buying until now then, playing utensils?"

"Oh Ajay... I'm referring to crockery to serve the food in."

"Ok, we'll shop for some on Saturday. Let's shift this lunch to Sunday," I said.

"But Ajayyy!"

"What happened? Don't do that; it scares me."

"We still have to buy cushions for the sofa..."

"Okay, will shop for the same on Saturday?" I sighed. "Any more shopping?"

"No, but Ajayyy! I'm just learning how to cook."

"Make only daal chawal, bread, one curry and a salad."

"Dal chawal! You're dumb or what? They are not coming to meet you. They are coming to meet me!"

I suddenly realized the big mess I was in.

"Bhavna, they are not used to being served lavishly. There were times when the three of us would eat from one plate. Don't take it seriously. If you welcome them like this, they will start coming every day," I grinned.

"Ajay, you are married now."

I didn't know what to make of that comment. But it was definitely not in my favour. *So, that is the problem.* I mentally cursed my married status.

"How many friends are coming?"

"Two. Hmm...no, three."

"You are not even sure how many friends are coming?" She almost screamed.

"The truth is there are two of them but they eat like...treat them like three people," I said like a beggar asking for one more chapatti.

"Of course, they're your friends. I'll manage," she sighed. "Ajay, I've to discuss two things."

Discuss? What were we doing for the past half an hour, singing a song? I thought. "What is that?' I grinned as if to say, *Come and kill me, I'm ready.*

"First, you have to clean the washroom. You never do that. Don't go in with dirty slippers. If I'm the owner of the kitchen, then you are the owner of the bathroom." *What idiotic logic is this?*

"Okay, agreed. Second one?" I said

"You have to fold your quilt after using it. You wake up like a king who has servants to pick up after him."

I smiled and nodded.

All scary after-marriage-life scenes flashed in front of me. I smirked. "Happy first month anniversary, ma'am."

Married life; bachelor friends

On Sunday afternoon, the doorbell rang.

"Bhavna, I think Vishnu and Harsh are here."

"Okay, open the door."

I opened the door, welcoming Vishnu and Harsh. They were school friends. Vishnu was a plump, simple-hearted fellow. Harsh had a French beard and was wearing a fat, golden chain around his neck, which must have been around 200 gms in weight. His thick, golden chain made him look like a rich bully.

"Hi Pandu!" Vishnu said.

"Hi, Gandu," I greeted him back.

"How are you, my jaan?" Harsh said.

"Fine."

"But we haven't come here to meet you; we are here to meet our bhabhi," Harsh said, settling his ass on the sofa.

"Okay, I'll call Bhavna."

I went inside. "Who is Pandu?" Bhavna asked

"Vishnu calls me 'Pandu' sometimes, out of love," I grinned. She stared deep into my eyes.

"Bhavna, this is Vishnu and this is Harsh," I introduced the devils.

"Hi, Bhavna," Vishnu said.

"Namaste, Bhavna," Harsh said.

"You people chat; let me bring something for my guests," she smiled.

"Bhavna, there's no need for such formality. We already had some paranthas around..."

I glared at Vishnu and interrupted him, "Don't be so formal. I already told Bhavna three friends were coming home." Bhavna stared at us doubtfully. After the introductions, Bhavna went into the kitchen.

"Saale kamine! She has been preparing stuff for you the entire morning," I whispered.

"We're not feeling hungry. We just had paranthas about an hour ago."

"Kamino, please eat whatever she serves you," I pleaded with folded hands.

"Saale phattu! Coward!" Harsh said.

"Next weekend, let's have a bachelors' party!" Vishnu said.

"But, I'm not a bachelor anymore."

"Tell Bhavna, my birthday is next week," Vishnu whispered.

"Okay, that's a good idea," I gave them a sly smile.

In the kitchen, Bhavna was making rotis.

"You need any help?" I said with a fake smile.

"These are your friends?" She whispered.

"What, now do I have to change my friends?" I said, shocked.

"Look at Harsh and his fat gold chain. He looks like some bully to me. And they use slang that I really don't like."

"What slang?"

"Pandu, gandu and kamine?" she whispered, furiously.

"Listen, they love me." I grinned. "Good friends don't believe in such formalities..."

"What do you mean? Will they address me as 'Mrs Pandu' or 'Mrs G'!" She responded, now furious. I kept silent. *Mr Pandu, you are in trouble*, I thought. "Ajay, I don't care what they say, but you are my husband and I don't like those words."

"Okay, let's have lunch first."

I dropped my initial plan, but my cunning mind that never gave up came up with another plan. I went to them.

"Listen, Vishnu, you have to invite me in front of Bhavna."

"Listen, Harsh, you have to appreciate the lunch," I said, pointing a finger at him. "Call her bhabhi. She will like it. Okay? Please!"

Both nodded, pitying the state I was in.

"The food was awesome, bhabhi!" Harsh said during lunch.

"Really!" she said, blushing. "Thanks."

"Ajay, next Saturday is my birthday, so are you coming for the birthday party?" Vishnu said, while looking at Bhavna. "Sorry Bhavna, it's a bachelors' party."

"Oh, that's perfectly fine. No issues," Bhavna said. I sighed in relief and nodded, accepting the invitation.

An hour after they left, I asked Bhavna. "So, Bhavna, what do you want to do next Saturday? Do you want to go somewhere? Shall I drop you somewhere? You'll get bored here."

"Don't you worry, I'll catch up on the serials I missed. It's only a matter of a few hours."

"Huh! Bhavna, this is a bachelors' party. It'll go on until two, maybe three o'clock in the morning. Harsh's house is in Shahdara. It'll not be possible for me to come back at night. I'll be back the next morning itself." I said Shahdara as if it was in the Sahara Desert".

"What will I do the whole night? I cannot sleep alone. I'll get scared."

"Scared about what?"

What a strange situation. My absence scares her and her presence is scaring me.

"I don't know about this, Ajay. But, I cannot sleep alone. You can come late, but please come back home."

"After the party, it'll not be safe to travel that late at night."

"Does this mean you plan to drink?"

"You know that I don't drink," I made a sad face. "Okay, I'll cancel it." I had learned how to execute Operation Emotional Drama before marriage, but it seemed more useful now.

"No, don't cancel it. But you are married, Ajay. You should be more responsible. Next time, show some decisiveness and turn down such invitations, you phattu."

If I listen to her, my friends will call me phattu. If I listen to them, she calls me phattu. God, please help me!

❖

Happiness comes with a price tag. Happiness had already been consumed the previous night. Now it was time to pay the price.

On Sunday morning, after the night-out party, Bhavna was silent. Her deep dimples had disappeared. She was not looking happy at all. She certainly had had a sleepless night. I started talking to an imaginary audience.

"All my friends are idiots! I'll not go for such a party again. I know that today they are bachelors but tomorrow they will get married and disappear," I said in order to lighten the mood, but I failed miserably.

"Is there any problem, Bhavna?" I asked as I hugged her. My question was like asking for directions from a blind man.

"I'm fine, Ajay; just leave me alone." She removed my hands from around her.

I know one thing; never leave your wife alone, especially if she says so. I decided to do something different. In order to please her, I thought I'd clean the washroom. I started pouring the cleansing acid all over the bathroom tiles and floor and began cleaning. My scrubbing and brushing created a lot of noise. I was deliberately making some noise in the hope of being granted some mercy in return.

After about five minutes, Bhavna came in, "What are you doing?" I was delighted! Maybe I was about to be granted some mercy.

"Cleaning the washroom," I said, proudly.

"I already cleaned it yesterday. There's no need to do it today."

"What!" It was as if she had slapped me. "It needs to be cleaned every day," I said in a firm voice.

"Do whatever you want. First clean your mind!"

She left. I hit the brush against my head and started brushing it.

She didn't talk much the whole day. I said that I was sorry a couple of times, but it didn't work. In my puja room, I found a picture of Lord Vishnu, lying on a snake and the goddess Laxmi pressing his legs. I talked to Lord Vishnu's photograph.

"Lord, are you enjoying this? Please tell me, where does a goddess like Laxmi really exist?"

Then I brought the picture to Bhavna and showed it to her.

"Who is she? I mean which goddess?" I asked, pointing at Laxmi's image.

"You're a Brahmin. I'm not," she said bitterly. All my efforts to please her had failed. Before sleeping, I made my last attempt.

"What happened, Bhavna? If I hurt you, I'm sorry for that."

"If ?" she asked. I shrugged. She turned her face away and said, "Leave me alone."

Finally, I gave up and decided to please her again the next day. I slept at around two that night. I felt as if my throat was being choked, as if someone was holding my neck and strangling me. Scared, I woke up gasping for oxygen.

"Bhavna, are you planning to kill me or what?"

"How heartless you are! How could you sleep when your wife is crying beside you?"

Crying? That touched me. "Oh, I'm really sorry if I hurt you, Bhavna," I said and yawned.

"Ajay, what are you sorry for? You just said sorry without even knowing what you are saying it for."

"Sorry, dear," I said.

"Another 'sorry'," Bhavna said.

"The last sorry was for not saying sorry for the proper reason," I added. I found what I was doing was quite unbelievable.

"What is the use of saying sorry?" She paused. I sensed that she was about to cry.

"Ajay, you are just saying sorry to avoid the situation without wanting to understand my problem," she said. And then she used her brahmastra. She cried. She was an emotional girl, but her bursting into tears was unexpected.

I hugged her and said, "I want my wife to be happy and cheerful. Whatever is stopping you from being normal, I'm sorry for that."

Sometimes, a silent hug works better than an apology. Finally, she melted into my arms and hugged me tightly, like a baby scared of something.

"Okay Bhavna, I will not leave you alone again. No more bachelor parties."

"Ajay, last night I couldn't sleep. My blood was boiling and it boiled further when I imagined that you were enjoying yourself with your friends. You can go for a party, but don't leave me alone. If a relative comes home, only then can you leave me. Or, you have one more option."

"What is that?" I asked, excited.

"Give me a baby."

"What!" I exclaimed "How is this party related to a baby?"

"Whenever you go for a party, I'll talk to my baby," she continued while hugging me.

"So, you'll complain to my baby about me?" I joked.

She laughed at that. I heaved a sigh of relief on seeing her expression change. She whispered one of the rarest words to come out of a woman's mouth, "I'm sorry, Ajay."

"Now, what is this sorry for?"

She laughed and said, "When women say sorry, you just listen. Some things happen rarely, so you should pay complete attention!"

My colourful life

After marriage, bachelor parties were no longer a feasible option. But, whenever I had an opportunity to party with my friends, I used it. My life demanded some newly-married friends.

At IERT, I had a roommate and friend Gaurav. His message about my illness had softened Bhavna after my proposal. It's time to introduce his wife Niharika. She'd been junior to us and was good looking and fashionable. Her once hidden desire to be a model was no longer hidden. Being junior to us, she used to call us 'Ajay sir' and 'Bhavna ma'am'. In spite of every love story being unique, both couples had a lot of things in common. We all belonged to the same college. We explored new places almost every weekend. I had a white Santro and it had contributed to many good moments in my married life.

One night after dinner, as a part of our daily routine, we went for a walk and talked. In order to burn some calories, we were roaming around a garden in my society in Noida. We'd already developed tyres around our bellies. Chatting and wandering around at night with your beloved is always enjoyable. No car horns, no disturbances, no escalation calls from office, nothing; just me and her. Only air rich in oxygen, and greenery all around us. But these walk and talk sessions were not always enjoyable.

"So, Ajay. How is your new company?"

"Yaar, HCL is a pretty good company and the best part about it is that Saturdays and Sundays are off."

"So, what is the plan for this weekend?"

"Plan?" We both laughed. The word 'plan' always had explosive consequences for us.

"Is there anything special this weekend?" I said, scared.

"Ajay, the coming weekend is the weekend before the second anniversary."

"So?"

"What is the gift? Are you planning anything?"

"Are you asking for a gift or snatching it?" I asked sarcastically.

"Everything changes when you're happily married," she chuckled.

"Yes, you are happy and I'm married. Everything is reversed," I joked and she laughed. "No need to hide your wish list, please, spit everything out," I probed. "But remember, I don't have a budget to gift a diamond, the way I did on our first anniversary."

"Are you scared? Am I a demanding wife or what?"

"If I gift you one again, then it will become a trend to give you diamonds every year."

"I'm not interested in all this crap. Actually I'm helping you, so that your confusion to get me an anniversary gift ends," she said like she was donating millions for a noble cause.

"It'll only be helpful if it's economical and cheap."

"Pandeyji, you're married to a queen. Have you ever seen me talking about money? So, be a little big-hearted."

"Mrs Pandey, you're married to a beggar who has to pay car EMIs, Flat EMIs, rent...." I said, starting to count.

"To hell with your dirty calculations," she said by opening her hair clutch. "How is my hair?"

"It's good." I shrugged

"Such a cold response," she said in a low voice. "Imagine me with coloured hair." She buttered me up further.

"Love you, Ajay. Actually, this is my anniversary gift. I wish to colour my hair."

I went blank, and I started trying to imagine my wife with coloured hair. The image of her as a blonde flashed in my mind. I said, grinning, "Bhavna, my mother will get a stroke after seeing her daughter-in-law with coloured hair."

"Ajay, this is an old desire. When I was a student, I postponed it because of Papa. Then I thought my husband would surely fulfil it."

"I miss your short hair."

"Ajay, if your mother saw her bahu with short hair, then?"

"Oh. Hmm...' I was speechless and confused.

"You know nothing about ladies' wishes."

"That's not true," I said, doubtfully. "I know everything about you."

"See my eyes; *yeh tumhe kisi ki yaad nahi dilate*? Don't they remind you of anyone?" She said coming closer to me and bringing my focus back.

"*Meri naani maa ki*," I said, repeating a Hindi movie dialogue and bringing in my maternal grandmother with it.

"You are a dumb husband. You never admire my eyes."

"Your eyes are pretty, why do I have to always say it?"

"You know, every morning when I go to office, do you know what Sonal says?"

I shrugged and she continued. "She says, 'Bhavna, *tumhari aankhe, yaar*, your eyes are so sexy, so deep. Just like Vidya Balan'."

I mentally cursed her. *I will kill you for this, Sonal.*

I stared like a goat, whose neck was hung and faked a smile.

"Listen, who will focus on Viday Balan's eyes? I mean she has other things to focus on, as well." I shrugged.

"Tharki! All men are dogs."

I gave up. "Listen ma'am, you're allowed to colour your hair with mehandi and if my mother enquires, just tell her it's the colour of mehandi and please end the matter or else..." I said in order to avoid further harassment.

"Or else what?"

"Or else this dog will bite you."

A loving daughter and
a would-be-father

On next Saturday, Gaurav and I were waiting outside the lounge of the beauty parlour and the ladies were inside their favourite temple, of course. The two married men were discussing the thing that haunted them.

"Yaar, how much does this hair straightening cost?" I asked.

"Ten thousand every six months," Gaurav said.

"So would colouring hair be a recurring cost too?" I asked, shocked.

"Yes, my dear. Be ready to invest at least ten thousand every three months."

"Oh," I said my mouth wide open.

"But, I'm worried about Niharika," he said.

"Why, what happened?"

"Last month only she got her hair straightened, and ladies sitting inside the parlour is like fire near to some explosives."

Gaurav's phone rang. Niharika was calling him inside and he came out five minutes later. Even a donkey could guess what had happened.

"Why are you so down?"

"As expected, Niharika also wants to colour her hair," Gaurav said frustrated.

"Oh," I groaned in support. "And what is the reason?"

"Reason!" he explained, "They are ladies. She wants it as Bhavna ma'am's anniversary gift."

"Excuse me? It's our anniversary and she is asking you for the gift?"

"Ladies can ask for a gift at any moment."

"Yes yaar, every month they want some lame excuse to shop."

"New Year, Valentine's week, Holi, birthdays, Karwachauth, Diwali...Christmas," Gaurav started spitting in frustration and I joined him.

"Anniversaries too. They even celebrate monthly anniversaries," I added. Gaurav frowned.

"Yaar, they can spend their whole lives shopping," he said and I patted his back in sympathy. And after ten minutes, Niharika came out.

"Niharika, where is Bhavna? Still colouring her hair?" I asked.

"No, sir, it's over. She's just checking out some gowns in the adjacent shop."

"Gowns!" I felt like I was about to faint. I looked into Gaurav's eyes.

"All the best, Ajay," Gaurav said.

I went inside and asked shocked, "Bhavna, if you are done, then what are you looking for?"

"Ajay these gowns are so pretty. I'm buying one for my mummy for her birthday gift."

I was haunted by the word 'gift' again. I started remembering my chat with Gaurav. She continued, "We gave her a gift last year, so she'll expect one this year too."

"So, this will become a trend?"

"Yes, giving my mom a gift and making it a trend, how excellent!" she said innocently. *Thank god she is not starting this trend for Papa, Pooja di, Nanhu and all the others*, I thought.

"Ajay, remember if I forget, it will be your duty to remind me to go on with this trend," she said.

Can we start a trend to not gift anyone anything, I thought of telling her.

"Okay, can we leave now?"

"Ajay, you're missing something."

"Oh, do I need to pay for it?" I asked, innocently.

"I've already paid for it. You're a dumb husband," she said. The words 'dumb husband' reminded me of Sonal's comments. It aroused me and I realized my mistake.

"Oh my god, your hairstyle is awesome. You know, you look just like Sushmita Sen."

"Get lost."

❖

At twelve o'clock sharp on the eve of our anniversary, we hugged each other.

"Wishing you a very happy anniversary, darling."

"Thank you, Ajay, and wish you the same."

I was looking at her when she asked me, "So, is there anything nice that you noticed after being with me over the last nine years."

"Yes, your eyes and stylishly coloured hair."

"Leave it, Mr Pandey. It took nine years for you to appreciate my eyes; you are such a *bhainga* husband...such a boss-eyed fellow."

"Ma'am, it's our anniversary night. At least spare me today."

"Today means?" she said with a dirty look.

"Oh," I frowned and went silent.

"I've one surprise gift for you and this is one of the best gifts," she said smilingly and I worried about how many millions of dollars had been burnt on it.

She switched off the lights and with the help of the light of her mobile, she inserted a USB into the USB drive and switched on our 32 inch LCD TV. After a series of clicks, a video called 'Ajay bhav Video' came up. Before clicking on the video, she came to me and I embraced her. We lay side by side waiting for the video to start.

"Do you know why this gift is the best one for you? Because it's free," she said. I smiled.

Then she played one of the best videos I had ever seen in my life: It started and a song from the movie *Yes Boss* played in the background:

Ek din aap yoon humko mil jayenge,
Phool hi phool rahon main khil jayenge,
Maine socha na tha.

And the caption that flashed read:

Cherish the journey of Ajay and Bhavna

A series of snaps were played one after another in a video montage. Bhavna had made a video with our best possible snaps. I gazed at her and kissed her. She was completely happy; her sparkling eyes glittered more than Vidya Balan's. All the snaps from our best moments in college – from her anchoring events, my mimicry, photos of Beena and our other friends, birthdays, snowfall in Shimla, our honeymoon in Kashmir, our favourite places, Karwachauth and photos from our wedding flashed on the screen.

The last line of the five-minute video made my day.

Forever yours...with lots of love, Bhavna.

After watching the video, I realized something; people always try to impress others with money, but the best gifts in life are always free. This is why Bhavna had countless memorable moments in her life. Because she enjoyed even the small things and I always cribbed about them. I remained silent. I was carried away seeing my memorable journey with my wife.

"Pandeyji, how's the gift?"

"Awesome," I said, hugging her, "but sorry for not adding any snap of any trip abroad."

"Trip abroad! I'm not at all interested in that. We've already explored the whole of North India. I'm now interested in having a baby."

"But our lives will have restrictions after we have a baby. We should go for at least one long trip," I pleaded.

"Ajay, I forgot to tell you some office news."

"Don't tell me Sonal commented on something that I hadn't noticed?" I joked.

She hit me playfully and said, "My company has offered me an onsite project in the USA for one year."

"Onsite for one year?" My mind started converting dollars into rupees and I was just about to start daydreaming when she stopped me.

"Ajay, come back from the USA. I rejected the offer."

"Rejected?! Why? It's just a matter of a year. The sacrifice of a year will lead to lot of money for us," I said moving away from her.

"I cannot stay away from my hubby for one year. And anyway, I want to have a baby in India," she said, hugging me again.

"I do, too, but..." I was about to say something when she cut in.

"Ajay, a baby delayed is a baby denied. I'm already twenty-eight and doctors say you should have your first baby before thirty."

"Yes, but, we still have two years. One year in America and the second year, a baby. Perfect plan," I said.

"Are you Vicky Donor?" She giggled. "Anyway, we are discussing this unnecessarily. I've already rejected the USA offer."

"Okay, dear wife, as you say. Now, tell me, whom do you want first? Aayushmaan or Pankhudi?" I said playfully.

"Pankhudi, of course," she said.

"Any specific reasons in wanting a girl child first?"

"Well, I was the second girl born in my family and my family was expecting a boy, especially my father."

"It's not a big deal, dear," I said consoling her. "Many people expect a boy and a girl in a family; even we expect the same."

"I know my father is very loving and caring, but he never shows his emotions the way Mummy does. You know, I've never seen my father crying," she said with respect in her eyes.

"If a person never cries, it doesn't mean he is not an emotional man. It could be that he is a strong man," I said covering her cheek under my arms. "The way he has supported our marriage proves how much he loves you."

"But sometimes you need to show your feelings."

"Don't you worry, ma'am. Maybe someday he will cry for you."

Bhavna was feeling a little sad. In order to cheer her up, I continued, "So my darling didn't receive much love. Come, I'll make up for it," I said while pulling her down to me.

"What are you doing?"

"Please, come and sit on my lap," I pulled her onto my lap.

"Ajay, I'm heavy." She resisted

After a few seconds, a five-foot-five-inch angel weighing sixty-five kilos with coloured hair and beautiful eyes was sitting on my lap. She looked like a cute, plump baby.

"So, my baby, you want love? C'mon, your husband will give it to you."

I played with her like she was a baby, pinching her cheeks and speaking by clinching my teeth.

"My baby, my laoo, my laaa, yaaaa," I said, making funny sounds.

"Papa milk," she said deliberately. *Milk?* I thought and put my thumb in her mouth and started singing a song that most Indian mothers sing to their babies: *"Chanda hai tu, Mera sooraj hai tu"*

Bhavna continued sucking my thumb.

"Thoda fatty hai tu, Thoda heavy hai tu..."

She burst into laughter and finally the atmosphere lightened.

"Ajay, I'll give you one compliment," she smiled and said emotionally. "You'll be a good father."

❖

Fictitious ending:

After a year, Bhavna and I were blessed with a beautiful baby girl. We were the happiest couple in the world.

For those who believe in perfect endings, I would suggest that you don't read beyond this. For all readers who believe in a perfect ending, my book ends here.

But, those who wish to explore the greatest lesson of my life should definitely read further, to learn my real ending, my destiny.

We all know, in truth, life is bitter; but truth prevails. You will turn the page, and I love you for this.

Bhavna's sleepless nights

Everything would change after we would have a baby. Between sleepless nights, an endless list of chores, and no time for yourself or each other, having a baby takes a toll on everything. In the first week of November, I had requested Bhavna to take a long trip with me before we tried for a baby. My desire to visit exotic places might be hindered after welcoming a baby into our family. With great difficulty, she agreed to go to Kerala. I booked the tickets for the first week of December.

Twelve days later, Bhavna developed a mild fever at around nine at night.

"Ajay, my body is aching."

"Have a Combiflam," I said, giving her a strip of medicine.

"Not Combiflam. It's a strong medicine. If I'm pregnant, it can have side effects," she responded, worried.

"Do you want me to take you to a doctor?"

"No it's not needed. Maybe it'll settle down by tomorrow. I'll have a Crocin. It's much lighter than Combiflam."

We went to sleep. At night, around one o' clock while I was sleeping and dreaming, my dream was interrupted by Bhavna shivering next to me.

"What happened, Bhavna?" I said, half opening my eyes.

"Ajay, I'm not feeling well. Please give me the Combiflam."

"What about the baby?" I smiled and gave her the medicine.

"Feeling-less husband; your wife is shivering with fever and you're busy dreaming about wandering in Kerala's houseboats," she said, swallowing the Combiflam.

I smiled and put a digital thermometer in her mouth. The thermometer reading got me worried. "Bhavna, it's 103 degrees. Do you want to go to the hospital?"

"Let's just wait till morning."

"Okay, as you wish darling. Your body is aching; do you want a light massage?"

"Just lie down and hug me."

I hugged her. I thought her body temperature might reduce by a fraction since mine was rising and we might reach an equilibrium.

"Are you feeling okay?"

"Yes. You know whenever I'm unwell and you hug me like this, it takes away all my pain."

I felt emotional by her words. To change the air I said, "I don't know about pain, but when I hug you, I definitely gain something."

"What do you gain?"

"My glory becomes glorified."

"Tharki," she hugged me tightly. Hopefully her tight grip was giving her some relief from her body ache.

"Can I give you a compliment?" I asked.

"Yes, you are always welcome to do that," she mumbled in pain.

"Currently, you are the hottest wife in the world and if you continue to hug me for the next hour, I'll be the hottest husband."

She smiled and her smile gave me some relief.

❖

The next day, we consulted a doctor but nothing changed. Her temperature continued to rise. After twenty-four hours, she was admitted to a private room at Prakash Hospital, Noida.

"Ajay, I won't come to Prakash Hospital for the delivery. I'll go to Fortis or Apollo," Bhavna said, lying on her observation bed. Whatever she did, only a baby came to her mind those days.

"Ma'am, babies were born even in the early days when there were no doctors," I said, continuing to stroke her colourful hair. I touched her cheek.

"Ajay, I'm sure when I get pregnant, you will take care of me like nobody else can," she said and smiled.

"Just rest and talk less," I instructed.

A general physician came in to check on her. He suggested a series of tests. After he left, she said in a worried tone, "Ajay, you've not told him that we're planning for a baby."

"So? He is a doctor; he could have asked."

"Suppose I'm pregnant and the treatment harms the baby?"

"Okay, okay. Don't panic. I never saw anyone so desperate to become a mummy," I said and went straight to the doctor.

Hiding my nervousness, I said, "Doctor, we're planning for a baby." Without listening to the whole story, he added one more test; a pregnancy test.

❖

That same evening, I got an emergency call from my office. I put on the TV and kissed Bhavna on the forehead and left.

I came back at around 7.00 p.m.

In my absence, she had had a chat with her mother. I don't know why they had taken everything so seriously, and had decided to fly to Delhi. She instructed me to book a pick-up cab from the airport.

"Why did you call them for such a small thing? They are old people; they shouldn't be given any trouble."

"Ajay, I didn't call them; they are parents, too. Now, don't worry. Just book a cab from the airport to the hospital."

At night around ten o'clock, Bhavna's loving parents entered the private ward at Prakash Hospital.

"You both are unnecessarily worried. She'll be fine by tomorrow," I said while touching their feet.

"I've told you many times, you're my son-in-law, you don't have to touch my feet," Bhavna's mother responded, drawing her leg away.

"See Ajay, I'm retired. I've lots of time," her father shrugged. "So let us devote some time to our children."

"*Aap toh apne app ko abhi bhi Amitabh Bachchan samajhte hain.* You think you're Amitabh Bachchan," the patient said.

"What does this mean?" Bhavna's papa asked, puzzled whether it was a compliment or a complaint.

"You rest, Bhavna." I explained to her papa, "She meant now you are old; you need to take it easy." He smiled.

It was decided that mummy would stay at the hospital overnight, and papa and I would go back home. After twenty hours, all her results were given. She tested positive for dengue hemorrhagic fever. It was a big relief because the doctors had not been able to diagnose what exactly was wrong until then. Her temperature continued to rise followed by body ache and vomiting. Her platelet count also went down. But while she tested positive for dengue, she tested negative for her pregnancy test.

❖

Bhavna's temperature continued to rise the next day. Her body and eyes had turned pale yellow. She vomited often and her nose started bleeding. She stopped eating and that turned her quite weak. She could not even go to the washroom by herself. She had severe headaches, and severe joint and muscle pain. I raised these points to the doctor.

"You need not worry; dengue hits badly for the first five to seven days. Her skin has turned yellow since her liver is affected and she is vomiting because of the same reason. We are hopeful that she'll start recovering within two days," the doctors pacified us and suggested a platelet transfusion.

Since Bhavna and I belonged to the same blood group, I donated platelets to her. My blood was infused with hers in a private ward and this further increased our love; however, it wasn't exactly what we had wanted.

"Now she'll recover," her father said.

"Any wife would be satisfied after sucking her husband's blood, so I think your thirst will also be over soon. Get well soon."

But that didn't make either of us happy.

The platelet infusion didn't end up being her saving grace; her temperature went on increasing and she became more irritated as well. The next day, she developed breathing problems. It was a weekend so I decided that I would stay with her so that mummy could get some rest. I found myself alone with Bhavna after five long days. "Ajay, when is this going to get over, yaar?" she said, holding my hand.

"No need to give up. If you do not start recovering tomorrow, we'll go to a better hospital," I said kissing her palm. After suffering from fever for six days, she was pissed off. I intentionally began talking about her favourite subject in order to distract her.

"Darling, if your parents come here for such a small thing, just imagine when you get pregnant, they'll definitely be with you even in the labour room."

Her face dimpled again. The word 'baby' brought her immense happiness.

"Yes, my baby will be taken care of by two mothers," she said with a sense of pride.

"Yes, two mothers; you and your mummy."

"No, then, three mothers since your mother will also not leave me alone," she said and smiled. "She asks about a baby every day. I'll be the first one to make her dadi."

"I know. Now rest," I said, stroking her head.

"But, Pandeyji, you are not Vicky Donor," she said. I smiled and kissed her forehead.

❖

I went to bed at around one o'clock. She called me to help her go to the washroom, so I woke up and helped her. Half an hour later, she called me again.

"Ajay, Come to me."

"What happened? Are you okay?" I enquired.

"Please give me a hug, Ajay."

I went to her bed and hugged her. But her liver pain separated us; I slept on her bed. Half an hour later, she woke me again and said, "Ajay, please help me to go to the window; I'm feeling suffocated."

I felt irritated. I hadn't slept for even one hour. But then I thought about how she'd been bearing the pain for so many days. How could I be frustrated the first night itself? I splashed water on my face and asked, "Are you not feeling well, Bhavna? Would you like to go outside?"

"Is that possible?" She puffed.

I left the room. Almost every staff member looked dead; only the emergency staff members were on duty. I found a wheelchair. I pushed it into my room and helped Bhavna into it. Bhavna was going out after five days. A staff member came to us. I pleaded, "She is fine, planning to get discharged tomorrow. She just can't sleep." He nodded and left.

"Are you okay, Mrs Pandey?"

"Yes, feeling okay. The world is so beautiful. I was inside a room for the last one week; it felt so gloomy."

"You know Bhavna, *Dabangg 2* is going to be released next month and one song has been filmed especially for you."

"And what is that?" she asked.

I lowered the volume and played the song on my cell phone,

'Dagabaaz re... Tore naina bade dagabaaz re...'

In those five minutes, I got my beautiful wife back. After five days of gloominess, pain and stress. But after a few minutes, her liver hurt and we returned to the ward. She slept; I could not express how satisfied I was. Even my sleepless eyes were pacified. It's lovely to see your beloved sleeping peacefully. Finally, she got a night's sleep after many sleepless nights.

Fight for your husband

Her situation worsened as she had developed severe abdominal pain, persistent vomiting and red patches on her skin. She still had a temperature of around 103 or 104 degrees. Her body and eyes had turned pale yellow. She vomited more frequently and her nose started bleeding. She'd become extremely weak and her legs were swollen. After six days of treatment, there was still no sign of recovery. She was almost panting for every breath.

We were worried because, according to doctors, she should have started recovering after six days. But her condition was worsening with every passing hour.

The next evening, we took the matter to the hospital management. We requested for a senior specialist, or transfer to a better centre. A senior doctor made the suggestion of shifting Bhavna to the ICU for further observation and care.

We asked clearly whether we should look for some other center and if everything was under control? But the doctor's response pacified us as they suggested a new set of tests. We decided to wait for one more day.

No one was allowed to stay in the ICU, which was painful for me; at least our presence had kept her morale up. As we were going to the ICU, I said to Bhavna, "We're just outside the ICU. You're being kept for observation only. If you will not start recovering from tomorrow onwards, we will go for some other hospital."

The next morning, she had started bleeding from her mouth. Her nose was blocked. She was breathing with her mouth and was continually thirsty. She demanded water every ten minutes. I kept putting drops of water into her mouth. She reacted like a little bird, when her mother brings her something to eat. It made me crazy as I could no longer hold my emotions. I decided to shift her for better treatment. The doctor arrived at around ten o'clock to have a look at the patients in the ICU. I interrupted the doctor for a discussion when he asked, "Are you with Bhavna?"

"Yes," I nodded.

"I'll call you in some time. I need to talk to you," the doctor said, worried.

After a few minutes, the doctor called us into a room. Bhavna's father and I went in to meet him. The moment I opened that door, I found that a team of four doctors was waiting for us, which scared me further. Somehow, the way doctors were staring at us increased my heart rate.

"In spite of taking every precaution, the patient is not doing well. Instead, her platelet count is decreasing further. She still has a fever and her liver function is still not improving," the doctor explained.

"These are the same symptoms as before. We know all this, doctor," I interrupted.

"The patient has developed an infection known as septicaemia. This can lead to sudden failure of all her organs. We've started a new antibiotic."

"How could she get infected when we had hospitalized her at such an early stage?" I interrupted.

"This is the after-effect of dengue; there are different types of dengue fever. Dengue decreases the immunity and in some cases, the patient gets infected from this."

"What is this septicaemia, doctor?" Bhavna's father asked.

"The root cause of septicaemia is a bacterial infection in another part of the body. Urinary tract infections, lung infections, and infections in the abdominal area are all potential causes of septicaemia. Bacteria from these infections enter the bloodstream and multiply, causing immediate symptoms."

"Is she in danger?" I interrupted, horrified.

"Patients with severe sepsis (not technically but typically, septicaemia and sepsis are the same) or septic shock have a mortality rate of about fifty to seventy percent, with the elderly having the highest death rates."

I didn't understand him completely.

"Is she in danger, please tell me?" I asked again, feeling dazed.

"The infection first attacked her liver and it'll continue to attack the other organs as well. In severe cases, one or more organs fail. In the worst cases, blood pressure drops, the heart weakens and the patient spirals toward septic shock. Once this happens, multiple organs – lungs, kidneys, liver – may quickly fail. The situation will worsen in the next twelve hours.

"The speed with which sepsis can turn fatal is often a product of the specific bug involved and the body's immune response to that bug. While not all sepsis is caused by bacteria, I'll use that example here. As the body detects and tries to respond to the bacteria, complicated chemical reactions occur between them that can cause the immune system to go haywire – toxic chemicals are released that cause tissue damage and organ failure. Once that process begins, it can be difficult to reverse it before sepsis kills the patient."

As he continued to explain the condition, he used a word no one wants to hear with regard to a loved one, "Yes, she is critical."

The word 'critical' felt like a slap to my face and I started getting goosebumps. I went completely blank and stopped listening to his explanation.

"What do you suggest?" Bhavna's father asked.

"If you can afford it, you should go to a better centre for further treatment," the doctor said.

"Which is the best hospital nearby?" I asked.

"Fortis Noida."

"Doctor, I asked you about this every day. Why didn't you refer her two days ago?"

He tried to explain. "Listen, son...."

But I left to see Bhavna. She was surrounded by green curtains. Her mother was there and they were chatting. I waited outside the curtain, listening to them.

"Mummy, give me a kiss. I'm losing hope now."

"My daughter, I'll give you two kisses," Bhavna's mother said. On hearing this, tears started falling from my eyes. I decided not to see her with teary eyes.

I broke down in tears, went to the washroom, and begged God, "Please save my wife. Please save her, God. Whatever mistakes I have made, punish me for that, but please save my wife..." I continued begging.

After half an hour, the Fortis ambulance was standing outside Prakash Hospital. "Papa, Mummy, you go in the ambulance with Bhavna, I'll come in the car." I instructed them.

We had lied to her about her actual condition. She was informed that she was being transferred for better care and diagnosis to recover soon.

Bhavna was brought out on a stretcher. She was pulled into the ambulance and I went inside as well. Bhavna's throat was choked. She was running out of breath; her mouth was filled with blood. I could never have imagined such a sight in my life. My emotions were at the top of the sky. I went to Bhavna and held her hand. I kissed her head; kissing her in front of her parents didn't bother me. I whispered in her ears, "Fight for me, Bhavna. Fight for your husband.

"I'll fight for my loving husband."

We were soon rushing towards Fortis. With every mile the ambulance travelled, I sensed Bhavna moving away from me.

You are the best wife

It is during times of crises that you can witness true human love. I'd never have realized that I was capable of loving someone in that way. Bhavna was sent to an emergency ward for initial observation. I continued holding her hand. Now nothing bothered me. I was only concerned for my wife. She was breathing with her mouth open and was continually thirsty. She demanded water every ten minutes. A nurse came to us, "We are shifting the patient to internal medicine ICU since she needs oxygen support."

Since only one person was allowed in the Fortis' ICU, Bhavna's parents waited outside. I walked along with her as she was taken in. I entered the ICU. It was a massive place, with around fifty beds and every bed was connected to a monitor which made a ticking sound. Three screens were mounted near every bed. The giant beds with the monitors looked like a dreadful three-eyed monster.

I continued holding her hand and giving her water. Tears were rolling from my eyes. I tried to hide them as much as I could, but failed miserably. I started stroking her head and cheeks compassionately.

"You'll be okay, Bhavna, don't worry."

Suddenly, a nurse ordered, "You cannot touch the patient with bare hands; she could get infected."

She gave me gloves and a plastic apron to wear. I put a glove on one hand and continued to stroke Bhavna with the other. I'd been standing there for two hours, and since it was time for a shift change, no one even forced me to go out.

"Ajay, your legs must be aching. Please go; I'll be okay," Bhavna said, panting. That was my Bhavna, regardless of all the suffering and pain, a lady like her could only think of others.

"You just rest. There's no need to say anything. I'm fine."

After fifteen minutes, a nurse interrupted me. "Sir, we need to start the treatment; you must leave."

"But I've to explain the patient's problem to the doctor. The patient is not in a position to talk."

"We'll call you once the doctor comes. You better leave now." I kissed Bhavna in front of the nurse, now nothing more significant in my life. "You fight here, I will fight outside. And remember Bhavna, you don't have to fight only for me, you have to fight for our baby also."

She smiled for a second and I left.

❖

A doctor soon came to check on her and I received a call from the ward. I went inside. The doctor asked me for all her details and said, "The patient is suffering from septicaemia and this is a multiple function disorder. Due to this every organ of the body starts failing. Her liver has almost failed. We cannot assure you of anything, but we'll try our best. The patient requires platelet transfusions; you've to arrange some donors immediately."

Platelets are parts of the blood that help the blood clot. They are smaller than red or white blood cells.

I folded my hand in front of the doctor and only manged to say, "Please save my wife."

"Don't do this, my son..Many patients recover at this stage, so all we can do is wait for a miracle."

I left the room in tears.

The same evening, Sachin and Ashish, Bhavna's friends from CSC gave me a list with ten people's names on it.

"Ajay, these are the list of donors and their numbers. They're ready to donate platelets."

I was going through the list but then I don't know why but they said, "Ajay, just give me a call whenever platelets are needed. We'll send one donor immediately. No need to carry the whole list."

It must have been evident from my face what I was going through. I was completely moved by their helpful attitude but could only manage to say, "Thanks, buddy."

❖

The next morning, since only one person was allowed to visit at a time, I went in to see my darling. Her body had swollen up further and she showed no signs of improvement. She was gasping for breath. Tears started rolling down my cheeks. I held her hand but didn't ask her anything.

"You'll be fine, soon. It's only a matter of a few days."

I tried to console her, but my eyes said that I was lying.

"Where is your mobile?" she gasped.

"Why do you want it?" But she insisted, typed a message, and showed me.

ur presence s hurtg me.

I stared at her. She intentionally turned her face away. I didn't say anything and left, rebuking myself. *You idiot, you cannot hold back your tears.* After I came out, Bhavna's parents visited her. Bhavna's papa called me.

"Ajay, don't cry in front of her. Bhavna was asking, why was Ajay crying?"

We had requested the doctor to not reveal anything to Bhavna, to keep her morale up, and she was not aware about the criticality of septicaemia. But, I think she has sensed the truth, because she was the one going through it.

"Sorry, Papa."

There were still a few minutes left before visiting hours were over. I went back inside to see her.

I went to Bhavna again and held her hand. "Sorry, yaar, I shouldn't cry in front of you." She continued to stare in the other direction.

"You know, Bhavna, I spoke to Paradise Holidays and they are ready to shift the date of our journey to January at no cost, but I cancelled the trip. I've decided to go to Venice with you and our baby, too."

She continued staring in the other direction. She was breathing heavily and her mouth was filled with blood. My throat began to tighten again.

"You know, babies travel free until they are three years old?" Despite my tears, I gave a smile, yes a fake smile, but my eyes weren't supporting me.

She called me close to her and said, "I'm okay, Ajay."

I broke down in tears, again, kissed her forehead and left. I continued begging God, "Please save my wife...Please save my wife..."

❖

Late in the evening that day, I received a call from the ICU.

"Are you with Bhavna Pradhan?"

"Yes," I said.

"Come into the ICU. The doctor wants to talk to you."

"Papa, the doctor is calling me inside," I informed Bhavna's papa, "Do come along."

"Yes, but if the doctor is calling us, it means it's a bad sign."

My heart was racing and I was flooded with emotions. Love, anger, hope and fear spinning together, sharpened by the nervousness I was feeling. After two minutes, we were standing right outside the ICU door; Bhavna was behind a green curtain. I made an assumption, *Has something bad already happened and did they call to inform us?*

ICU doctor came to meet us.

"Who is Ajay?"

"I am," I said, and he handed me a document that needed to be signed. I signed it with a lot of suspicion, but without asking too many questions.

"What is the significance of this?" Bhavna's papa enquired.

"Are you her father-in-law?" The doctor asked.

"No, I'm her father."

I knew he was going to tell us some bad news.

"Listen, you have to be brave and calm. I want to inform you that Bhavna's condition is deteriorating further and we're planning to put her on a ventilator."

I felt numbed. As these icy words pierced me, it felt as if my blood was freezing. Bhavna's papa asked, "Does this ventilator mean that it's an emergency?"

"No, she is only being put on the ventilator because she is not able to breathe properly. Her kidneys and heart are both in danger."

"What are the chances of recovery?" I asked bluntly.

"A rare chance, I will be truthful. This document is permission to put a patient on a ventilator; once she is doing well, we can remove her from that, but her condition is getting worse. The ventilator is not the problem, the problem is the infection."

He continued to explain something but I had stopped listening to him. My mind was only on Bhavna. His words were surely falling on my ears, but they were not being processed by the brain.

"So, is she not on the ventilator yet?" I asked.

"No," the doctor said.

"Can I see her?"

"That is why I called you. This ventilator will only be removed once she starts recovering or there are signs of improvement. She'll be administered anaesthesia which will make her unconscious so that the ventilator doesn't cause any damage."

"What if there are no signs of improvement?" I asked.

"Then I'm sorry..." he sighed, "It's possible you will be talking to her for the last time."

I stared at Bhavna's papa. We both understood.

"Papa, do you wish to see her?"

"No, you go. I'm okay," he said. I understood. No one in the world would want to see his daughter dying.

But I could not control myself. I wanted to see her badly, but what would I say to her? It might be my last chance to speak to her. I thought I would hug her, feel her, but this would give her an idea that something was wrong and she might break down completely. Surely, there was something I wanted to say, but I didn't want to lie to her and tell her she would be okay soon. With a heavy heart and this dilemma in mind, I went to her.

I was thinking about what to say to my darling while tears fell continuously from my eyes. I felt that Bhavna was slipping away from me. My heart was beating fast, my lips were dry and my emotions were at their peak.

I went behind the green curtain. The most beautiful woman in the world lay choking and gasping with her mouth open and red blood was visible around her lips. She lay with her mouth open and her eyes closed. It was the most horrifying moment of my life. Watching her struggle to breathe made me insane. I wished I could have given her my breath and part of my life, but I was helpless. I had never felt so helpless in my life.

I started kissing her hand and then I kissed both her beautiful, dimpled cheeks. I touched her eyes and mouth; she opened her eyes and looked at me. I kissed her forehead. With great difficulty I said, "I love you, Bhavna. And you are the best wife."

She mumbled something. I put my ears close to her. She collected her strength and whispered with ragged breaths, "I love you too, Ajay. And you are the best husband."

Her words released my dam of tears. I kissed her forehead again, and left immediately. I went outside, hugged Bhavna's papa and cried like a baby. My mind stopped working and I continued to sob. I don't know how Bhavna's papa was able to keep calm, but an unlikely thing happened that day. Bhavna's papa cried, in front of me first time and said, "My loving daughter! Oh God, why my daughter, God...why me, God?"

I had a mental conversation with Bhavna.

Bhavna, see. Today you changed your father. He cried and cried for you. You were wrong; he is not a tough man, he is the most loving father. Do you know why your name is Bhavna? Bhavna means 'feelings' and that is why your father named you so.

The world is beautiful

"Listen God, my wife doesn't deserve this end. Please save her; don't put her through so much pain. Please help me, God. I'll dedicate my whole life to others, but please save her. God, if you save her, you'll find me a changed man. But if you continue putting my wife in pain, I promise that I'll never respect you again in my lifetime." I went to the Sai Mandir in Sector 61, Noida and begged God.

That day, I was just as silent as Bhavna. I only spoke to God. I was alive, but felt like my soul was on a ventilator. The next morning, my father called me and enquired about Bhavna and me. First time in my life I said, "I am missing you, Papa."

I went numb, and he could sense the pain in my words. He was frightened by my behaviour and assured me that he would soon be coming to see us. Pooja di was also on her way to Delhi. Almost everyone who loved us started coming to Delhi.

I received a call from an unknown number late in the evening. "Are you with Bhavna Pradhan?" The question haunted me. *Should I put this on an answering machine or what?*

"Yes," I said.

"Please come to the accounts department."

I reached the department.

"Sir, your hospital expenses have overshot your medical insurance limit. The medical insurance limit of ninety thousand that was available was used up on the first day," he said.

"No, but I had a higher medical limit," I said.

"Maybe the rest of the money was used up at Prakash hospital," he guessed.

"What is the bill right now?"

"Around four lakhs," he replied.

"Four lakhs? You mean one lakh each day?" I said, shocked.

"Sir, the patient is extremely critical and on ventilator. You'll have to pay some money immediately."

"If my limit was used up on the first day itself, why are you informing me after four days? Today is almost over and tomorrow is Friday. There is only one day left to arrange money. Half the financial lenders don't work on Saturdays and Sundays and even my office is closed on those days."

"Sir, we understand that there was a delay in communication, but your account is now in the escalation zone."

"What does that mean?"

'Sir, you have to deposit something or....'

"Don't you dare stop the treatment. I'll deposit one lakh tomorrow and the rest will be deposited on Monday," I said furiously.

I saw everyone and everything that tried to come between Bhavna and me as my biggest enemy. Now we were fighting two fights; one was Bhavna's fight for her life in the ICU and the second was my struggle to find funding and donors for her platelet transfusion.

I was not concerned with finding donors for her platelet transfusion since Bhavna's CSC friends, especially Sachin and Ashish, had already taken charge of that. Whenever I called them, they sent a donor immediately. My heartbeat wasn't raised by the demand for money; in fact, I was aware that I didn't have much money. A lakh in a day was almost impossible to arrange, but I was calm and cool. I felt like I had already been through the worst. The next day, I called one of my friends, Sanjay, who worked at HCL with me.

"How is Bhavna?" he asked right away.

"The fight is on. No improvement yet. Listen, Sanjay, there is a funding emergency."

"I had already discussed this with Jaipal (my boss). He said that if any help is required, do not hesitate to call him."

He sighed, "Today is Friday, however, so don't expect any financial help before Monday."

"Don't worry. You just do your part. I cannot allow money to be an issue for me and my wife."

"Can you write an e-mail to him?"

"Okay."

I went straight to my car which had been parked in the Fortis parking lot, brought back my laptop and started typing.

Dear Sir,

My wife Bhavna is suffering from a blood infection commonly known as septicaemia. She has been hospitalized since 21/11/2012 first at Prakash Hospital, and has now been transferred to the ICU at Fortis Hospital, Noida.

This occurred due to dengue. As a result, all the other body organs were severely damaged. In addition, lung and liver problems have resulted in her being put on ventilator for the last three days. As per the doctors, the situation is critical and we need all your support and prayers.

Since Fortis Noida has been providing their best services, the medicine and other expenditures are costing approximately one lakh per day.

Looking for special help and consideration from your socially responsible organization on the grounds of humanity to extend financial help to her. In this crucial time, a generous response will be like God's blessings.

Looking forward for a helping hand and your prayers.

Regards,
Ajay Pandey

After writing the email, I was planning to call HDFC Bank for a personal loan. Meanwhile Bhavna's father came to me. I explained the whole situation to him.

"Ajay, yesterday I received a call from Bhavna's boss, Reema. She also asked me to reach out for any help, if required." Bhavna's father had been using her mobile.

Bhavna's papa called Reema. She asked him to write an e-mail to her and she assured us she would try to help. I dispatched another copy of the same mail to Reema.

❖

On Friday evening, the doctor called me to update me on my darling's conditions. Bhavna's papa and I went to the doctor. He continued to spit poison.

"She is not doing well but she is not deteriorating further. She is still critical."

He went on to explain about platelet counts and heartbeat readings, but my mind had stopped processing anything.

"What are her chances of recovery?" I asked bluntly.

"Few patients recover from this at this stage, but don't ask about chances. For the patient, either it's hundred percent or nothing," the doctor said.

"Suppose, she deteriorates further, then how many days do we have?" Bhavna's Papa asked.

"I have no answer for this," the doctor answered.

"Suppose she starts doing well from now, then?" I asked.

"Yes then," the doctor sighed, "she has to be here for the next thirty days." I introspected, *Thirty days means thirty lakhs!*

❖

We were definitely going to have to arrange a lot of money. Bhavna's Papa and I began discussing the matter. "You also arrange something, Papa."

"I have already arranged something. It'll come by Tuesday. But how much money will be enough?"

"As much as possible. Papa, I'll fight till her last breath," I said with moist eyes. *I will not give up.*

"Relax beta, I understand." He patted my shoulder lovingly.

"Tomorrow, Papa, Maa, Didi and Monu will also be coming, so you have to arrange for visiting passes. One more thing, please guide Monu with regard to the blood bank formalities since two donors will be coming for platelet extraction tomorrow."

"Are you going somewhere?" he asked inquisitively.

"I will be going to Nehru Place. I had opened a locker to keep Bhavna's gold jewellery..." I couldn't say anything more as my throat began to tighten again.

"So, are you going for a gold loan?"

"Yes, Papa. But I don't feel embarrassed selling any of my things, if it gives us any hope for Bhavna's recovery."

"I totally agree with you. How much is that gold worth?"

"At least three lakhs."

"Means three days more," he said.

❖

Once I reached the bank, I received a call from Harsh.

"Ajay, where are you?"

"Yaar, I'm at the bank to withdraw my gold," I answered.

"Planning to sell gold for money?" he asked, shocked.

"Either sell or mortgage."

"How is Bhavna? I'm at the hospital and wanted to see her."

"I'm sending Monu's number. He's my younger brother. He'll guide you. I'll talk to you later."

After collecting all the gold, I made my way to Mutthoot Finance at Indirapuram. I had reached halfway when I received another call from Harsh.

"Ajay, where are you?" Harsh enquired.

"I'm on my way to Indirapuram."

"Want to meet you, urgently," he insisted.

"Ok, hmm...we can meet in front of Headstrong since that will be on my way."

"Give me a call, I will be waiting there."

After thirty minutes, I parked my car opposite the Headstrong office. Harsh came.

"Ajay, kamine! Why didn't you inform me?" he asked, furious.

"Yaar, yesterday was your wedding. How could I?"

"Kamine, my bhabhi is in trouble and you're talking nonsense," he shouted and hugged me. While hugging he put something in my hand and said, "No need to say anything and no need to return it."

I was shocked by his action. I opened my hand and found his thick gold chain sparkling in my palm. Tears started rolling down my eyes. I hugged him back.

"Saale, everybody will think that we are gay," he said. I remained silent and continued to hug him. He went on, "Please go Ajay, and please..." he said with tears in his eyes, like he was a hero.

I smiled and said, "Saale, *pakka shaadi main dher saari mili hogi.* You must have got many of them at your wedding."

I left and didn't say thanks, since it would have meant nothing compared to his kindness. He was a true friend. I texted him, *One day I will return some of it and I love u.*

Hope this is a better way to say what I wanted to:

Thanks Harsh Tomar. The world is beautiful because of friends like you.

The world is beautiful...indeed!

The patient was not doing well. The doctor sang the same old song. Whenever I went to the ICU and saw the tubes going into her mouth, I felt like I would burst. I went mad seeing the machines take over a human. I used to touch her palm and kiss on it.

But it was less painful for me comparatively when she was on ventilator support. At least she was calm, not struggling for every breath. I stopped saying much. Now all our relatives, my parents, Pooja di – everyone was there. I was a bit relived physically, but the mental storm still kicked my nerves. I wondered how I would deal with these things that seemed like they could only happen in the movies. Helplessness and hopelessness started overcoming me. I was hoping for a happy ending like all those movies where everything gets resolved in the end.

Sometimes, I tried to negotiate with God like a businessman, presenting him with counter offers. And sometimes I begged like a beggar too. Every day, more relatives and well-wishers came and prayed in their own ways.

One of my relatives had given me auspicious ash from Shirdi. I had never believed in any of these things in my life. But now I believed in anything and everything that could bring Bhavna back. I applied that to her head myself. If someone had asked me to kill the Prime Minister of India to get my wife back, I would have done it without giving it a second thought. No matter what I was doing physically, internally I was begging to God to please save my wife.

On Saturday afternoon, I was alive but something had died inside me.

A beautiful five-year-old kid had come up to me.

"Mausaji," Nanhu said. I hugged him and kissed his cheeks.

"Mausaji," he inquired. "Where is Mausi?"

"Mausi is not well, she is sleeping," I said. He looked innocently confused.

"What did you bring for her? Doremon, Ben 10 or Angry Birds?" I asked with great difficulty.

"Mentos candy," he said, handing me a small box. I remained silent and looked at it.

"I want to give this to Mausi," he insisted.

"Mausi is sleeping, Nanhu," I sniffed. I couldn't say anything else to him.

"Nanhu, come here." Pooja di shouted. He started walking towards her and then he came back and said, "Mausaji, you keep the Mentos."

❖

The same day, in the evening, the doctor called me. I requested Bhavna's papa to attend to the doctor since I had a severe headache. I was fed up of listening to the same old tape record. I cried almost every hour. I used to sit and think of the past; it felt like she wanted to say something. My ears started receiving her voices and due to intense pressure, my head started troubling me. Bhavna's papa came back and started explaining reports, which showed her platelet count and her blood pressure, but I wasn't listening.

"Is she improving?" I asked, "Is there any hope left?"

"The situation is getting worse. Now it's not in their control," he said.

I closed my eyes and started thinking about Bhavna and talking to her.

❖

My father came to me and started discussing about going to better centres. Someone suggested Medanta Hospital and someone else suggested AIIMS. My father also wanted to discuss the same with me, but I refused as I had lost all my abilities to talk and think.

My father and father-in-law started talking about what to do, and now my father started looking for ways to shift Bhavna to AIIMS. Getting an admission into AIIMS, especially for a patient in such a critical state, was almost impossible.

The next day, my father found a connection to Salman Khurshid, the then foreign minister, but was unable to reach him. The minister's secretary gave us a letter requesting for Bhavna to be hospitalized at AIIMS. But the hospital management at AIIMS was used to receiving such kind of letters. They refused on the ground of unavailability of beds in the ICU. My father didn't admit defeat; he tried to reach the top management of AIIMS via the Prime Minister's office. My father was not very resourceful; it was the people who wanted to help us. After herculean efforts, my father managed to get a bed at the AIIMS ICU.

On Monday morning, I received a call from Jaipal Singh, my reporting manager.

"Ajay, how is your wife?"

"Not well, sir. We're planning to shift her to AIIMS."

"That would be a better choice. Listen, I had a word with the HCL HR; they're going to talk to you soon. Please tell them about whatever funds are required and, listen, don't worry about how to return them. You just focus on her recovery."

"Thank you, sir."

"No need, dear. If you don't receive the funds soon, just give me a call. All the best. We are all with you." I thanked him from my heart and murmured, "You are a real boss."

Bhavna's boss Reema also came to the hospital to see Bhavna and assured us of financial help. My father called me to shift Bhavna to AIIMS. After turning this impossible thing into possible, we were all hopeful. I mentally pleaded, "Bhavna, the world is so beautiful and people are so kind. Please come back. Please come back, darling. I don't want to live without you."

The biggest truth of life

We reached AIIMS hospital. For the first time I realized why private medical hospitals are running successfully and the condition in which India's best government medical centre was. But, it was more than a temple to me; this was my only hope. I reached AIIMS hospital in my half dead condition and a junior doctor came to me and asked for the details of the patient's medical history. This was the first time I had spoken in the last three days. I sounded like a pre-recorded tape.

"How are you related to the patient?" he asked. Again, I seemed to realize that he was going to utter a bitter truth that I didn't want to hear.

"How does it matter to you?" I said frustrated.

"In the last ten years of my career, I've never taken a patient into the ICU in such a critical condition. I just wanted to know how you got her here."

"Then you should speak to my father."

"No, it's not required. "

"Doctor, what are the patient's survival chances?" I asked, hoping against hope but he too sang the same old song.

"Very slim," he said. I mentally yelled, *Fuck you. What is the use of you being here!*

Outside the AIIMS campus, my father came to me. He took a long look at my half-dead state, my eyes protruding and my body barely upright. He suggested that I should go back and rest and offered to stay back at the hospital that night.

❖

4 December 2012

Early in the morning, Bhavna's papa and I headed towards AIIMS in my Santro. Bhavna's papa was hopeful.

"This is a sign, Ajay. She will recover from this."

"What is the sign, Papa?" I asked as I drove.

"Getting a bed in the ICU at AIIMS, in such a condition is... is a miracle," he said.

I said nothing but his words definitely increased some RBC count inside my anaemic state. I needed to hear that badly and it hardly mattered whether it was true or not.

We reached AIIMS. I called Papa to come down and take the car away, letting him know that I would stay there till nightfall.

"Papa, come down. I'm waiting just near the emergency gate."

"Park your car in the VIP parking lot and come into the ICU," my father said in a serious tone.

"What happened Papa...?" I asked, stiffening in fear.

"Just come, beta. Remember Sonu, you are my brave son."

I didn't say anything. I disconnected the call and took the Lord Ganesh idol from the centre of the dashboard, threw it outside and started crying uncontrollably. I felt like I had lost everything. I shouted, "From today, there is no God for me. I'll never respect you again in my life. I hate you."

I shouted at God. The kind of language I used that day, I had never even used for a human being. I started feeling choked. I drank half a bottle of water and then, with a heavy heart, I walked to the sixth floor.

Since there was no chair outside the ICU lobby, I settled on the floor itself without bothering to check if it was clean or not. I leaned my head against the wall, closed my eyes and waited for that harsh, clear sentence that no one wishes to hear in life. Papa called someone on the phone and said, "Bhavna has left us."

Tears started running down my cheeks. I had never wanted to hear that, but that was the truth of my life. My whole life started flashing in front of my eyes. My struggle to make the marriage possible, how determined I had been, the vows we had taken together, all the happy moments of friendship, our love, our fights – all the emotions flashed through my mind like a superfast film.

Nothing was in sync in my mind. Tears poured down my eyes. I clenched my fist hard while clenching my teeth and mentally fought with God. *God, if I die tomorrow, please send me to hell. If by some mistake, I land up in heaven...if I get a chance to face you, believe me, I will take revenge against you for the injustice that you've done to me. Today, not only has my wife died; today, you have died. There is no God for me now.*

I started feeling suffocated once again and went to the balcony. I leaned over the wall and started staring at the ground. A stream of dangerous questions came to my mind:

If I jump from here, how long till I'm declared dead? Can these doctors save me? What is going to happen just after death? Is there life after death? Is Bhavna here to watch me, and if yes, then I should jump so we both can be together... two souls perfectly in love.

I don't know from where Bhavna's words came back to my mind. I remembered what she had said when Vaibhav's girlfriend had committed suicide.

"Ajay promise me; you'll never commit suicide in your life...no matter how difficult the situation might be."

"Why would I commit suicide? I have a beautiful person like you to share my life with."

"Whether I'm with you or not, if you lose interest in life, start living for others."

Tears were still flowing down my face. I had never surrendered. That day, I gave in and surrendered. With a heart full of pain, I spoke to my Bhavna. I spoke to a part of my heart that had been taken away from me.

"For whom, Bhavna? For whom should I live? You were everything to me," I cried. "I surrender, Bhavna. I surrender...."

I felt a pair of fat hands on my shoulders and I turned around. It felt as though Bhavna had answered my questions through my father. I hugged him and started sobbing like a child. A few minutes ago, I'd only been a husband, but my father made me realize that I was a son too.

"Don't you worry, Papa. I'll not commit suicide."

"I know, you are not a coward."

"When exactly did it happen, Papa?"

"Early morning, at seven. Her heart stopped ..." He paused. "Do you want to see her body?"

"No, but don't call it a body."

I refused to think of Bhavna like that. "Papa, I don't want to use the word 'dead' for my wife. She will always remain alive in my heart."

"She'll remain in our hearts always, as the most beautiful chapter of life."

Nine-and-a-half years of friendship and love cannot be called a 'chapter'. I had a mental conversation with God, *God you tried to delete the most beautiful chapter of my life. I will write a book and will make Bhavna immortal in those pages.*

Her hurting presence

At noon at the Lodi Cremation Grounds, a big statue of Shiva, painted in blue, was standing tall at the entrance. 'The biggest truth of life is death.' Slogans similar to this one were painted on the walls of the cremation centre. I had never been to a *Shmashan Ghaat* or cremation ground before. Even here, it was not as silent as I had imagined. The sound from the traffic nearby was breaking the silence. I settled down in the middle of the ground, completely uncomfortable, ignoring everyone. Many familiar faces were staring at me but my mind went blank. I didn't pay attention to anyone.

Bhavna had laid alone inside the ambulance, wrapped in a white cotton sheet. It reminded me of how she had fought with me when I had gone to a party with Harsh and Vishnu without her. *How could you sleep alone, Bhavna, how could you?* I mumbled.

I noticed someone standing with a baby. The sight took me back in time.

On the morning of our second wedding anniversary, I was half asleep after the late night baby drama act. My sleep was interrupted by loud music from 9XM. My sleep had already been disturbed by multiple phone calls. Our parents were calling to wish us. Four different people called and each had the same things to say. The first was wishes for the happy anniversary. The second was to work against the government policy of population control.

I left the bed with great difficulty and went to the source of the commotion. I found a dancing curve inside the kitchen with beautiful hair playing with the utensils in the kitchen. I went near her and wrapped her in a hug.

"Good morning ma'am, and wishing you a very happy anniversary, again," I yawned, as she moved to dance with me.

I asked, "Darling, how'll you dance when you conceive?"

"My baby will also dance with me," she giggled.

"Ma'am, your baby would not only dance, with the MRF tyre-like tummy you've developed, the baby will swim as well."

"Not my baby, our baby. And yes, it'll swim and slide like swooooooo!" she whistled.

And suddenly the phone rang. Bhavna whispered, "Pooja di's call."

After five minutes of thank yous, crackling and laughter, Bhavna brought the phone to me.

"Wishing you a happy anniversary, Ajay," Pooja di wished me.

"Thanks di."

"Now Nanhu is asking for a sibling to play with," she said.

I groaned silently. After marriage, the only thing the whole world had to say was, "When are you having a baby?"

After attending to the call, I lay on the bed and started thinking. How a baby would change our life. After the baby, there'll be no holidays, no honeymoon. Only responsibility. The whole room will smell of urine, with nights of broken sleep, no peace or quiet. Nothing. 'Ajay, you're trapped, my friend,' I murmured.

Just then, Bhavna entered the room with tea. To distract myself from all these scary thoughts, I focused on the TV and an advisement flashed on the screen:

'Johnson's Baby Kit, complete baby care.'

After watching the ad, I stared into Bhavna's beautiful eyes. She noticed my dazed expression, smiled and said, "What happened, Pandeyji?"

"Nothing... I'm just thinking about how a baby will change our life. After a baby, there'll be no roaming around, no nightlong parties, no weekend masti, and no movies at the cinema halls."

"Exactly, Pandeyji. So the baby is going to make us realize all that," she smiled. "How our parents sacrificed their happiness at every moment of their lives..."

I felt touched by her words but I went over to the other side of the coin. "Bhavna, may I ask one question seriously? Will you answer from the heart?"

"Please go ahead," she frowned, concerned.

"Tomorrow, when you become a mother, will you start loving the baby more than me?"

"I love you a lot. I feel special that you don't want me to share your share of love with anyone."

"Can you please answer me?"

She thought for a while and asked, 'Tell me, today...whom do you love more, me or your mother?"

"I love both of you equally," I played it safe, to avoid any emotional drama.

"That's not a fair answer; I thought I would score more," she said in disappointment. "Now what would have been your answer if I'd asked you this question five years ago?"

"Of course, my mother would be on top of my list," I answered quickly.

"Correct, Ajay. Even if someone asked me today, whom I love more, my mother or you, my answer is you. But yes, five years ago, my answer was not the same. So, when time passes, preferences change. Enjoy the present and super enjoy tomorrow," she said.

I was speechless by her explanation. I was about to enter into deep thought but was interrupted by a sweet voice, "Pandeyji, you'll not feel *jealous when we have a baby with eyes like mine and your smartness. Some parts of the baby's face will match mine and some will match yours. And when you hold that hybrid piece of Pradhan and Pandey in your arms and when he smiles, in that special moment you'll forget everything. Maybe, you'll start loving the baby more than me."*

I went silent and smiled. After a minute, she came closer and said, "Ajay, one day I will be on top of your list and you will say, I love you the most."

"I'll love that day." I smiled.

My thoughts were broken by the sound of the wood and flames in the cremation centre. A human body was turning into fumes.

Initially, I thought I would not see her, but the fumes from the cremation centre had created an intense sense of insecurity in me. I went into the ambulance and locked its door. My father opened the door and tried to sit with me. I requested him, "Papa, please leave me alone." He left without protesting.

Now, I was sitting with my darling in a closed ambulance. I lifted the white sheet, placed my hand on her bare body, and said, "Bhavna, I've a compliment for you. You are not the world's hottest wife, darling. Now, you're the world's coolest wife," I cried.

I tried to look at her face and lifted the cotton sheet. It was the worst thing I'd seen in my life. I'd never imagined a beautiful face could be in such bad shape. I pulled down that sheet immediately. My whole life was starting to flash in front of my eyes. I shouted at my cold wife, "Wake up, Bhavna. I just want to say that...I love you even more than my mother. You are on top of the list...but I don't love this day."

I was in a flood of tears. I cried at the top of my voice and kept repeating my question. "Bhavna, how can you leave me when I'm in trouble? Bhavna, please come back!"

I buried my face in her stomach and shouted. "Where is my baby?" I kept on weeping inside the ambulance. But all my questions, complaints and pleas had fallen on deaf ears. I could hear my unanswered questions ringing in my ears after touching that cold wife that lay in the ambulance. I touched her cheeks, eyes, hair, kissed her on her forehead and said, "I'm sorry for not giving you the chance to be a mother."

In my mind, I heard a sharp comment, '*A baby delayed, is a baby denied.*'

After one hour of rituals, a wonderful human being, a beautiful lady, a best friend, an obedient daughter-in-law, a caring daughter, a would be mother, a lovely mausi, a loving sister, a rib-tickling bhabhi and the world's best wife – all these women-in-one had been burnt by me. After lighting the wooden logs on which my silent Bhavna was lying, I turned my head away. I didn't have the courage to see my darling turning into fumes and flames.

I murmured, "Your presence is hurting me."

Love makes us secular

After seventeen days of worrying, praying, anguish and struggle – everything became colourless. I had not only lost my wife, I lost my confidence too. The losses took up one side of my heart. On the other side, my rage, at destiny and God was slowly increasing.

At home, everything reminded me of her. Small decorative items in the room, the kitchen articles, my bed, car, the Scooty, and every corner of the room. Each and every object imbued with the presence of Bhavna. I was not comfortable in my own home for the first time. My colourful life had become black and white. Whenever I closed my eyes, I felt that Bhavna was standing right in front of me. I started sleeping more and the whole flat remained silent. There was no sound for hours. No 9 XM, no music, no dance and no playing with utensils. No more jokes to giggle on.

When a beloved leaves a family, it brings some changes. Some are obvious and expected, and some are unbelievable.

After three days, the funeral ceremony or *shradh* was over. It was decided that all of Bhavna's belongings would go to her sister, Pooja. I kept all her used dresses with me, though, maybe in a crazy hope that she would come back someday. It was madness to expect that Bhavna would come back again, but I still felt she would.

Bhavna's bags were searched for anything important. In the process, I found some idols. That was it! The anger that had been stored up inside me, exploded like a volcano. Right then, I decided that there was no place for any idols at my home. I started throwing away images and idols of gods.

My mother came to me. "Sonu, what are you doing?" she asked worried. "These are not toys."

"No, they're not. They are garbage."

"If you don't want them, please give them to me," she said and began collecting them in a big white plastic bag.

Her words had no effect on me. I began to look through Bhavna's purse for any important documents. In one of her purses, I found a photo hidden in between her credit cards. It was in a plastic bag. I opened the bag. It was a picture of a famous lord who I would prefer not to name. I threw it away that instant.

"Sonu, why are you throwing away all these things? You are disrespecting Bhavna," my mother said. I glared at her. She continued, "All this that you call garbage, belongs to her. She bought it and kept it." Then holding my hand, she added, "You never believed in God."

Her words shook me. I picked up that picture, put it back and mumbled.

"God, sometimes you should learn from human beings, too. Yesterday, you took Bhavna away from this beautiful world and look, today she saved you. If she hadn't brought you here, you would be floating inside a gutter."

I gave all the religious items to my mother and said, "Maa, please take them away."

After two hours, when everyone had gone, Maa and I were the only ones left inside the room. She was sitting on the other side of the bed, holding a sari. I recognized it. It was the sari that was gifted to Bhavna by her when she had first come home after marriage. She buried her face in the sari and began to weep at the top of her voice. She kept repeating two words,

"*Meri bahu, meri bahu...*"

Her uncontrollable sobbing was moving. For a moment, I almost felt like she was Bhavna's mother; she was a mother crying for her lost daughter. I sat there helplessly. I had never seen my mother weeping like that. I crossed the bed and went to her. My blood was boiling with frustration and helplessness. I hugged her. She broke down further.

"Everything will be fine, Maa," I said. But she continued to sob without a moment's pause. "Why are you crying, Maa? You didn't lose anyone. Your son is still alive," I said as an idiotic suggestion but had nothing else to say to cheer her up at that time.

"How can you say I didn't lose anything?" She said, still hugging me and sobbing.

"What have you lost, Maa?" I smirked. "She was a Kayastha girl. Your Brahmin son is still alive."

My words burnt her. She left my embrace, glared at me furiously and slapped me hard. Last time when she had slapped me, it was ten years back. Then she shouted at me.

"Don't insult her. She was neither Kayastha, nor Brahmin. She was my loving bahu."

I felt touched by her words. I hugged her back and wept and thought, *Love makes us secular.*

On behalf of Bhavna

I continued to be confined within my house. Now my relationship with Bhavna was one-sided. Every day I would wake up in the morning and say, 'Love you,' and, 'Miss you'.

Millions of thoughts popped in and out of my head every day. Yet, all questions remained unanswered.

What is the purpose of my life? What is next? How do I go on with life?

Another part of my mind tried to answer. The condolence calls kept coming from across the globe. Soon, I stopped talking to everyone.

One evening, almost eight days after the storm, I opened Bhavna's Facebook account and found a number of hateful messages about that villain, God.

God takes those whom he loves the most. May God give your family strength. Rest in peace.

Every time I read anything about God, it ruined my mood. I logged out of Bhavna's account and logged into mine. Once again, I found an explosion of crappy, sympathetic messages about the villain. On that day, I realized that when a wound is too big, then no such messages will help heal you. Nothing had been able to end my inner turmoil. After a few minutes, I found a message from one of my friends from IERT.

Dear Ajay,

I heard about the tragic incident in your life and was truly shocked and shattered. Bhavna was a gem of a person and I know the loss is irreparable but I urge you to find the strength and give life a tough fight.

These are trying times. I'll pray to God to give you enough strength to endure them. I know how you must be feeling; our partners are our greatest strength and they inspire us, but fate takes its own course.

You were so lucky to have Bhavna in your life. She was really a star and always kept everyone around her happy. Cherish the years that you spent together and just be strong. Support her parents and do the things that she loved. Fulfil all her unaccomplished duties and desires, you'll find a strange satisfaction in this.

I'll always pray for you and will miss Bhavna, too. I'll cherish her memory forever, as I loved her.

Take care, Ajay, and let me know if you need any help of any kind.

Neha

This message transported me to a different world.

Support her parents and do the things that she loved. Fulfil all her unaccomplished duties and desires, you'll find a strange satisfaction in this.

Neha may have only written to comfort me, but it was by far the best consolation message I had received. These words had given me something to live for.

Yes, I had to accomplish all her unfulfilled duties and desires but what were her unaccomplished duties? She wished to be a mother but I could not fulfil this wish now; I could not be a mother.

My mind started working overtime to find the best ways to fulfil her unaccomplished goals.

I found my answer. I had to take care of her parents, especially her mother. A mother who had two children; one of whom had had to leave in the middle of life's journey. Yes, that was the most difficult part of her life.

I talked to my Bhavna, "Bhavna, now everything I do is for you."

I went straight to the top right corner of her Facebook homepage and found a birthday reminder. I went to the profile of the girl whose birthday it was and posted this on her timeline, 'Wishing you a very happy birthday, on behalf of Bhavna.'

Two broken people;
one unbroken promise

How was I going to make someone else happy? I had been thinking over and over about calling Bhavna's mother. As much as it was on my mind, it was extremely difficult for me to call a mother who had just lost her young daughter.

Yet, I picked up the cell phone. I was about to dial, but questions hung over my head.

What shall I say? What can I say to her that would make her feel better? What should I say so that my words may heal her wound? How should I try to console her?

In my mind, I was having a desperate discussion with myself. Maybe I didn't know what to say but a few things were now clear to me. I was not going to say that we were helpless. Or that God wanted us to be brave. Or that this had been destined. The phone was still in my hand. With courage and strength, a broken husband called a broken mother.

"Hello mummy, Namaste."

"Ajay! Khush raho. Be happy."

"How are you mummy?"

"Same as you," she said.

"I'm completely okay."

"If you're completely okay, then I'm also completely okay," she said. I paused for a few seconds.

"Mummy, you've to come out of this. Pooja didi told me that you're not talking to anyone," I said.

She went silent and I continued, "Listen Mummy, we all are sad and we cannot help it."

I didn't have any logic to reason with her. I didn't want to leave the situation the way it was by saying that God is great; he might have a great plan in store. I refused to leave myself at the mercy of some power, whose existence meant nothing to me.

"It'll take some time, beta. Slowly, slowly I'll learn to accept this," she said.

"But Mummy, the way you are behaving, it's not just slow, it's the slowest way of handling something," I protested, gently.

"Bhavna used to speak to me daily. I am trying to find my bearings but whenever I'm free, I miss her...." She broke down.

Don't you worry about the void, Mummy. Now, I'll be talking to you daily, I thought.

"Mummy don't you worry, after sometime, we'll get used to it. Please try to involve yourself in something," I suggested. "Maybe in some social activities? If you busy yourself with the well-being of others, you'll feel happy for sure."

"We've decided that on the fourth of every month, we'll donate a meal to the orphanage," she said and her words reminded me how Bhavna had celebrated our one month anniversary.

"I'll tell you about something beautiful that happened on our one month anniversary on the fourth of August. Bhavna had bought a cake for the celebration. This scared me and I asked, 'Ma'am, are you going to celebrate every month or what?'"

I narrated the sweet memory in detail and my tears started flowing. I had to stop talking to hide the pain in my voice.

She replied, "She chose the fourth of July for her wedding and God chose the fourth of December to take her away." I hated God even more.

"Forget God and destiny, Mummy. It's like peeling open an onion; the more we peel back the layers, the more we cry. And we're not going to get anything out of it. We don't know why this happened to us. But when things are beyond our control, we're not supposed to think much about it. Now, tell me, when are you coming to Delhi?" I said, in order to change the topic.

"No, I'll not come to Delhi."

"I can understand."

"But you can come to Raipur," she said, sobbing softly.

"Mummy, don't you worry. I'll come soon."

"Ajay, please don't end our relationship."

"I didn't get you, Mummy."

"You'll always be my son-in-law."

"Mummy, what are you saying?" I wanted to convince her that I had no such plans, but she added, "Don't end our relationship, Ajay. This relationship was created through her."

"How can I end something that was created by her?"

I started calling her daily from that day onwards. There were days when I didn't talk to my mother but never did I skip calling my mother-in-law. I booked a ticket to go to Raipur for Holi. It was heart breaking to go to my wife's home without my wife. But then, I was going for her.

❖

Every morning, I awoke long before dawn and lay exhausted and wakeful, with eyes closed, thinking the countless days I still had to live without her.

I decided to resume my office after ten days. On the first day to office, as I was all set to start my vehicle, I stared at the balcony. Tears rolled down my eyes as I realized that there was no longer the person who used to throw me flying kisses. Death might have consumed her body, but her soul always lingered with me. She continued to occupy the seat beside me when I took the car for a drive. She accompanied me on my evening walk. She cried with me when I watched a romantic movie with a tragic end, sharing my popcorn. Sometimes, I wondered why I don't meet with an accident so that I could find a place in the world she was in. Then, when I thought about how her parents had mourned her demise, I realized it would be the same case with my parents too if something happened to me.

My wallet still had her photo with boyish crop cut hair. Every day, I talked to the photograph, she was still smiling, as if saying, "Pandeyji, please get another photo. I have long hair now."

Whenever I saw a couple walking hand in hand, it reminded me of the reality that there was no hand to hold mine. All funny messages related to a wife were no longer funny to me. There were days when I played loud music, closed my eyes, switch off the lights and felt like I was dancing with her. My mind was dancing, lips were smiling and eyes were raining.

All through the isolation, anguish and pain, I had two friends who never left me alone. One was my washroom mirror which dared to face my idiotic questions. It was the only thing that witnessed my tears and frustration. My second friend was her velvet pillow which let me imagine it was her. I used to hug the pillow every night and talk about the events of the day. I wished the pillow could talk back.

The quality of life is
what matters

Bhavna's mother called me and cried over the phone. But I was unable to console her. I felt helpless. After the call, I buried myself under my quilt, closed my eyes and started talking to Bhavna.

"*Bhavna, how do I help yaar? I'll not admit defeat against destiny or God; I'll fight against this. Bhavna, please suggest how I can help?*"

I started reading the Hindu religious text *Gita*, but I gained only two messages from it. One, the soul is immortal and Bhavna would be reborn on earth; I appreciated this. But the next moment I found that we human beings are helpless and that everything is destined in advance by God due to some previous karmas. I hated the book after that; I refused to read it again.

I started watching motivational videos by Sri Sri Ravi Shankar, Swami Vivekanand, Shiv Khera, Robin Sharma, Sandeep Maheshwari and many more, but they failed to motivate me.

Holi was nearing and I was to meet Bhavna's parents. I was compiling all Bhavna's videos on separate hard drives because they were priceless to me now. I played Bhavna's last video; she had made it on our second anniversary. While watching it I noticed a photo in which we were enjoying a shikara ride at the Dal Lake in Kashmir. It reminded me about what Bhavna had said regarding her ideology of life. I remembered the conversation and felt motivated.

On Holi

Your wife's maternal home is normally the best place to celebrate Holi in India, but when you don't have your beloved with you, even a merry festival becomes meaningless. The moment I entered the house I saw a big collage mounted on the wall. It had photos from her childhood till her marriage and after, and on the top was a quote:

Dearest youngest, will reside in our hearts forever.

Every part of the house and every article somehow had the sense of belonging to her. Now my wife's maternal home had turned into a painful place to stay. At night, I talked with Bhavna's parents.

"Papa I wanted to show you something."

"What is it?" Bhavna's papa enquired.

"A video Bhavna made as an anniversary gift."

Now everybody was expressionless, as the person responsible for all our expressions was no more. I played that video. I intentionally switched off all the lights in the room. As I knew what was about to happen, I lay down near them.

The video began with music in the background:

'Ek din aap yoon humko mil jayenge.
Phool hi phool rahon main khil jayenge,
Maine socha na tha.'

And the caption that flashed read:

Cherish the journey of Ajay and Bhavna.

A series of pictures were played one after another in a video montage. Bhavna had made a video collecting our best photographs. Only Bhavna and I were swaying to a song in the entire room with her invisible presence. All the snaps from our best moments in college – from her anchoring events, my mimicry, photos of Beena and our other friends, to birthdays, snowfall in Shimla, our honeymoon in Kashmir, our favourite places, karwachauth and photos from our marriage flashed on the screen.

That five-minute video came to an end with the following lines:

Forever yours...with lots of love, Bhavna.

After we had watched the video, I switched on the lights. Needless to say, we were all in tears. It was ironic; just seven months back that video had been a reason for me to smile. Now it was responsible for my tears. Bhavna's mummy started making her way to the washroom. I stood in her way and hugged her. We broke down and this relieved me. Bhavna's papa too had broken down and he went away to the other room.

"Mummy, don't hold back your tears. The more you cry, the lighter you will feel. You'll be less burdened with grief and pain. When we restrict ourselves and don't cry, we actually build up internal pressure. And when the tears fall, the pressure is released," I philosophized.

Bhavna's mother continued sobbing and then went quiet.

"Mummy, tears don't help that much that you turn crying into a lifelong activity," I made a feeble attempt to joke.

"I don't want to cry, beta, but when I realize how short my daughter's life was, and how she could not enjoy it, it breaks me..." she said, sobbing again.

"Who said your daughter did not live well or did not enjoy life?" I freed her from my arms. "Now, I'm going to say something your daughter said."

I continued, "Tell me the best moments of your life. For example when you got married, when you had your first baby, when Papa got promoted, when you bought your first car or something like that."

"I don't understand, beta," she said.

"How many memorable moments can you remember in your life?" I asked seriously.

"I have had a tough life, Ajay. I don't have many good memories," she said.

"Now listen carefully, Mummy, you don't even have some good moments after living for sixty years and if I ask you how many sad moments you have had in your life, you might score a century. If someone asked Bhavna the same question, she would have said she had more than a hundred happy moments and a few bad moments in her life.

"Mummy, she lived for a fewer number of years but not in terms of moments. This video and its every picture is related to one such moment and many more that she did not even capture, but cherished throughout her life. Please understand, Mummy. Life is not measured by the number of breaths we take, but by the moments that take our breath away.

"Life is a journey; we all are born and will die someday. Some celebrate their silver jubilees, some celebrate golden ones and some may score a century, but life cannot be evaluated on the basis of the number of years spent alive. The quality of life is what matters, not the quantity."

She remained silent and after absorbing my thoughts she felt relieved and said, "The only relief in my life is that my daughter was happy."

"Your daughter will be remembered because she was always the happiest soul and she made others happy, too." I sighed. "I want her mother to be a happy soul like she was."

She hugged me back and cried. After that, she smiled and nodded.

I had been controlling my tears for the last few minutes, I went straight to the washroom. I felt choked and my throat was dry. I opened the tap so that my sobbing wouldn't be heard outside the washroom's brick walls. My sobs were masked by the noise of water falling from the tap. I stood in front of the mirror, twisted the tap, and crossed my arms hugging myself, imagining her. I closed my eyes, cried and kept murmuring in frustration,

"I can't do all these things alone, yaar. Why did you leave me alone like this? Missing you..."

But every time I cried, I heard a sweet voice in my mind, which said,

Love you, Ajay. And you are the best husband.

The right thing for
the right reason

*W*hat *is the aim of my life? Why am I earning? What is the real reason for happiness? Should I earn more money? But for whom? Life is uncertain. What happens if I die tomorrow? What'll happen to the money that remains unused? Why had all this happened to someone like her?* These were the questions that kept striking me. I lost interest in my job and money and concluded that real happiness never comes with wealth. I started finding the true purpose of my life.

Few weeks after Holi, I moved from Noida to Indirapuram, in the hope that a new place might bring some new memories and keep away the painful ones. My old utensils were unpacked again. I was sharing the flat with two roommates. I returned to bachelorhood. By then, my mother had gone back to Rihand Nagar. Once again, I was alone. Almost all my friends were married by now, so while they had sympathy for me, they had limited time. Earlier, even a small achievement brought me happiness, but now even small troubles frightened me.

I was still searching for a reason to be happy. But I strongly believed that only a happy person could bring happiness to others. So I felt it was my moral duty to keep myself happy.

One day I was driving to Connaught Place. It was an ordinary day. Delhi was humid and boiling hot. I stopped my car at a red signal near the ITO crossing. On my right side, I saw a middle-aged man on a bicycle with two small kids sitting behind him. One looked around five years old and the other around two years old. The one riding the a bicycle must have been the father of those poor kids. They were tied down with a small rope so that they don't fall off while he was cycling. I turned my head and smiled at them, but they didn't reciprocate. I opened my window and waved my hand to get their attention. The older kid smiled and waved back, but the younger kid remained inattentive.

The traffic light timer said seventy-two seconds and was counting down until it turned green. I don't know why I wanted to see the younger kid smile. First, I thought of giving him some coins, but coins would be useless to the kids and it might have insulted their father. I started searching for something else, but couldn't find anything around me.

The timer displayed thirty-one seconds and counted down from there. I opened the glove compartment of my car, searched, and found a box of Mentos candy. I was surprised and wondered where it came from, but then I remembered Nanhu had given it to me to give them to his Mausi. Without further delay, I handed the box to the younger kid. Both looked extremely delighted. Meanwhile, the light turned green and I shifted into first gear. The younger kid smiled, waved and the older kid joined him. I waved back at them.

I smiled back and felt a sense of weightlessness. It felt as if I had landed on the moon. It was the first time my soul had been happy after six months of agony, tears and pain. I felt joy in my veins that made me think this must be true happiness from the heart. After a long hunt for a valid reason to remain motivated about life, finally I received my life's most meaningful lesson from two little kids. They were the real motivational gurus for me.

Tears started rolling down my cheeks as, I said, "I've found it, Bhavna. I found that true happiness in life lies in helping others."

❖

I started looking for an NGO via Google, where I could devote some time to others, something that would give me happiness. By accident, I found www.saikripa.org. I went to the website and found that it was an orphanage and then I clicked on its 'contact us' section.

SAIKRIPA, Address: Z-133-134, Sector-12, NOIDA-201 301, U.P., India.

Registration Office A-153, Sector-21, Jal Vayu Vihar, Noida-201301 UP, India

That orphanage was close to my office. I called the given number and said, "Hi, I'm Ajay. I want to dedicate some of my time for the students."

"You can come anytime between 4.00 and 6.00 p.m.," the lady on the other end of the line said.

I went to Sai Kripa and realized that I had gone past it at least a hundred times before, but had never noticed it. I met with one of the workers there; her name was Seema.

"Hi."

"Hi, you wish to donate anything, sir?" she enquired.

"Actually, I don't have money but I have a lot of time. Can I give them my time?"

"Yes, you can donate your time. You can help the children with their homework or with English grammar," she answered.

"Thanks, Seema. But where are the students?" I asked.

She took me to an open area which was attached to a big sewage canal. There was a foul smell coming into the garden. The walls looked extremely shabby with many company posters displayed on it; maybe they wanted people to think of their organizations as socially responsible. Around twenty kids were playing in the ground. Some of the students were studying in small groups monitored by a tutor. *I will be one of these tutors*, I thought.

"Sorry to ask Seema, but are all these kids orphans?"

"Yes, all of them," she answered seriously.

"This one-year-old girl was found in a dustbin at the Noida City Centre," she said. Her words hit me.

"This is Neena. Her parents died of cancer. Everyone here has a story, sir."

Tears filled my eyes, but I controlled myself and asked, "What about you? Are you working or...?"

"I am one of them," she said. I was numb for a while as a storm swept my mind. She called out, "Sooraj and Neha, please come here." Two kids came up to her.

"Say 'Namaste'!" she instructed.

"Namaste, uncle," one said. The other said, "Namaste, Bhaiya." I smiled back and started hunting for my happiness.

"Namaste, kids. So, I'm your new tutor," I said.

"Ajay Bhaiya will help with your English homework," Seema instructed them. I thought, *Poor kids, they will have a horrible teacher.*

"Please open your bag. What is the homework for the day?" Seema asked with authority.

Both opened their homework books. Suraj was a bit annoyed since some of the kids were playing and he eagerly wanted to join them.

"Bhaiya, will you come every day?" Suraj asked, worried.

"Suraj, I'll complain to Mummy," Neha said and glared at Suraj.

"Mummy?" I exclaimed, surprised. *How could orphans have a mummy?*

"Rajagopal Mummy," he answered. I was still confused.

"Neha, don't stop him from asking anything," I said to Neha.

"So Suraj, do you want to play with them?" I asked, teasingly.

"No, Bhaiya. Normally people come here for a few weeks, then they get bored and leave in the middle. So I'm confused about which book to open."

His words felt like a slap and left me with millions of unanswered questions.

"Don't worry, Suraj. I'll come on weekends only," I said.

"Okay, bhaiya."

My words had soothed him.

"Neha and Suraj, you can play with the others. I'll come again next weekend."

"Thanks, bhaiya," they said in unison and ran away. I wanted to clear my doubts so I went straight to Seema.

"Seema, you said all these are special kids, but I found them calling someone 'Mummy'."

"They call our head functionary Rajgopalji Mummy."

"So everyone calls her 'Mummy'?" I asked, surprised.

"Yes, including me and the staff. She is the only mother we have," she said.

"What about her own family? I mean, what about her own kids and husband?"

"She is over fifty years old and single. She devoted her entire life to these children." Seema's words shook me.

"She didn't have any children, but look, today she is the mother of sixty kids," I mumbled.

"Do you want to meet her?" she asked.

"No, not today. Maybe next weekend."

"So, will you be coming every weekend?" She smiled. I understood why she was asking questions like this. I smiled back and said, "Maybe."

"Sorry to ask you this, but why are you giving us your time?"

"Everyone here has a story; you will get to know mine someday."

I started my car and headed towards Indirapuram. I was completely silent, but there was a wave inside me.

I lament my loss; how are these children happy after losing everything? If they can smile, why can't I? How has she dedicated her whole life to them? Do these kind of people exist? You are such an idiot; life has given you everything but you always crib.

And I spoke to my omnipresent beloved, "Bhavna, today I found a temple of humanity and God, too. I'm sure this God is better than your fictitious one. I'll write my story and whatever I earn, I'll donate it to such a temple or maybe I'll create such a temple for humanity. My love for these kids is more than my hatred towards God. Now, let's begin the right things for the right reasons."

I can forgive, but will
never surrender

I found this story on Facebook:

A tigress lost her cubs due to premature labour. Shortly after, she became depressed and her health declined. She was later diagnosed with depression. Since tigers are endangered, every effort was made to get her back to health. Zoologists disguised piglets in cloth with tiger prints, and presented them to the mother tiger. She now loves these piglets and treats them like her own. And, needless to mention, her health is back on track. Yes, we all have feelings.

I started writing my own story; my story of love and happiness. And yes, you are reading the same. And I realized that I have had a happy life. All my moments of happiness and struggle made me realize that I was not the only unfortunate person on this earth. Every moment I cherished with Bhavna came back to me, and while writing, sometimes I laughed and cried, too. It's like I was reconnecting with my beloved wife. And now I have a different perspective of my fortune. Maybe I had lost the most beautiful person in my life, but the nine years with her felt like nine centuries.

My outlook on life became positive, but my anger and disrespect towards God continued to grow.

Her mother's birthday was around the corner. The fourteenth of September.

I was planning to fulfil my wife's unaccomplished task.

For her mother's birthday, I bought a sari as a gift. Birthdays or celebrations hold no meaning in life when hearts are shattered. But I was firm because I had to keep this trend going, as it had been initiated by Bhavna.

I couriered the sari to Raipur with a letter that read:

Hi Mummy,

I know I'm not here to hug you and kiss you. But I have my agent in Delhi who'll accomplish my tasks of gifting you things and wishing you on every occasion.

But whenever I see you from here, I find you people crying and weeping for me and it hurts me. You know, I'm happy here. I'm the youngest and the most beautiful one here and everyone feels jealous of me.

Now, I want my return gift and I know you won't refuse.

There are two kinds of personalities. There are those who have everything and still complain as if they have nothing. And there are those who lose everything and act like life has given them everything. I know you belong to the second category.

Enjoy life so much that others are jealous of you and give them a shock that you are still alive and inspired to live further.

Wishing you a very happy birthday, Mummy.

Wear this sari on your birthday, if Pandeyji has couriered it on time.

Your loving daughter,
Bhavna

On 13 September, a day before her birthday, my phone rang. The screen said, 'Bhavna's Mummy calling'.

"Hello, Mummy."

"Thanks, beta. I received your courier and thanks for the sari," she said, sobbing.

"Oh sorry, Mummy my gift had..." But she interrupted me.

"No need to be sorry, my son," she said and I was touched to be called 'son.' "I was lucky to have a daughter like her."

"I know, Mummy."

"Listen son," she interrupted. "It is the worst possible thing for a parent to see their daughter going in front of them, and they are just seeing it with helplessness. It may be true that I had a tough life, but that was not the only thing I had. I was blessed with two beautiful daughters. We cared for them, nurtured them, and raised them like sons. But today, I can proudly say that if anyone has a daughter like her, they don't need a son." She sighed. I was silent and felt my heart breaking.

"Look at what she did. She left us in the middle of the journey but..." she sighed. "...Now, I feel like I am blessed with a son."

I don't know whether she was the tigress, but I always tried to be a piglet. She had given me the best compliment of my life; a mother who had lost her daughter thought of me as her own son. It broke me and tears started pouring out of my eyes. I felt choked. I lost my voice, but didn't want to break down in front of her. With great difficulty I said, "Mummy, I'm getting a call from office. Will call you back."

I disconnected the call, went straight to the washroom and cried. After two minutes, I wiped my tears, splashed water on my face and had a glass of water. Still I felt suffocated but I had to call her back or she would guess that I was crying. I called Mummy back.

"Hello, Mummy."

"Is your official rap over?"

"Yes."

"You are a liar. Don't hide your tears, beta," she said. I smiled but remained silent."But, you deserve more from life. We're your well-wishers. We don't like to see you cry just as you don't like seeing us cry."

"I'm happy. I have two mothers now," I said, clearing my throat.

"But you'll be happier when you forgive everyone. When we are angry, we carry a huge burden on ourselves."

"I have already forgiven everyone. The insect that had bit her, the doctor, my fortune, everyone, including myself," I said in a low voice.

"What about God? Have you forgiven Him?"

"I will never forgive Him for this. He will never get my respect again," I said firmly.

"Son, forgiveness is the attribute of the strong. Forgive God and show that sometimes humans are even superior to Him."

"He is nothing for me," I said, furiously.

"Forgive others, not because they deserve forgiveness but because you deserve peace."

"No, Mummy, he has taken away the most beautiful gift of my life."

"If he is responsible for your loss, then God is the one who brought her into your life." She sighed. "Forgive him for all the things that life has given to you," she said and her words forced me to think deeply.

After a few seconds, I said, "Will try, Mummy."

"I have another request. It's almost a year. Now you have to start your journey, again. You have to marry again."

"People will laugh; a mother-in-law is asking her son-in-law to marry again," I joked.

"I'm not your mother-in-law anymore. The law cannot make a bond like we have."

"You know, nowadays everyone is talking about this."

"All these people love you."

"I know, but enough gyaan for the day."

"Okay bye, son."

"Bye, Mummy." We hung up.

After the call, I felt like crying. I closed my room door and drew the curtains. It was a cloudy day, but for me, it was already raining for the last so many minutes. I turned 9XM on and increased the volume of the TV. It was a deliberate attempt not to be noticed by my roommates. While lying on the bed, songs played but I was lost in my own thoughts.

How did life give me such a nice partner and wonderful moments? How unfortunate those orphans at Sai Kripa are who don't have a mother. I have two mothers. What a wonderful life and what an extraordinary journey of nine-and-a-half years I have had with such a loving soul. Throughout my life, I had been counting only what I had lost, but in that moment, I realized what I had.

Bhavna's cell phone beeped to signal a text message, but I was engrossed in my agony.

"God, you don't deserve my anger. Today, I'm forgiving you not because of anything bad you did. I'm forgiving you for all the good things you have given me. But you'll not earn my respect again. No more, thanks. Both sides are balanced."

I felt relaxed and happy but tears were still pouring from my eyes.

I picked up Bhavna's cell phone; Sonal (Bhavna's CSC Friend) had sent a message.

It's crazy to msg you like this Bhavna, but just wanted to say that I'm expecting a baby and am missing our chats about babies. Missing you yaar.

Now that word 'baby' hurt me.

I opened my cupboard, searched for Bhavna's shawl, and lay on the bed. It still smelled and felt like her. I covered my body with her shawl, hugged my pillow and started crying. When we decide to quit, a voice comes from within, the voice of the one who loves you.

A voice inside me said, *Ajay, you cannot surrender like this.*

I murmured, "I will not."

And an old thought came up - *Whether I am with you or not, if you lose interest in life, start living for others.*

I thought, *How can a human being in love surrender himself? I thought I will not surrender. I'll fight and fight till the end. For myself, my family, her family, for others and, most importantly, for Bhavna.*

I started speaking to God.

"God, one last favour. If you grant me this, maybe I'll start respecting you again. If I ever get married again in my life and am ever blessed with a baby; I want a daughter first. She should have beautiful eyes, dimpled cheeks, coloured hair and...and Bhavna's soul," I closed my eyes and started negotiating like a child. "Even if you fail to give me these things, just give me Bhavna's soul back in the form of my daughter. Give my Bhavna, please, give my Bhavna back...I will not surrender..." I kept on praying in tears.

But my cunning mind popped up a doubt, "Mr Pandey, how are you going to recognize her? How will you know that your baby is Bhavna?"

This reminded me of what she used to say when I used to pull her up on my lap and play with her like a doll. I smiled in spite of my tears. The worst kind of pain is when you have smile and tears together.

I said with certainty, "I will recognize my Bhavna, God. I will. Since whenever I say 'I love you, my daughter', she will smile and reply, 'I love you, too. And you are the best father'."

Bhavna Pradhan. Born on 8 November 1983.
Became Bhavna Pandey on 4 July 2010.
Always alive in our hearts
Love you, Bhavna. And you are the best wife.

Acknowledgement
(Bhavna Speaks)

How can someone rest in peace, when they have a crazy husband like Ajay. But still, thank you Pandeyji for giving me an opportunity to write here.

I was not blessed with enough time to fulfil my duties. I am obliged to thank many wonderful hearts who had been kind enough at various stages of my life.

Thanks to my lovely childhood friends: Swati, Tarun and Bharti for making my childhood happy and memorable. My moments with you guys are cherishable always.

Sincere gratitude and love to Beena, Neha, Umaam, Akshata, Niharika, Anshul, Ashish, Dipendra, Arvind and Gaurav for making my college days fruitful and meaningful in all ways.

Sonal, Sheel, Sachin, Mayank, Ashish, Rashmi, Namita, Shwyeta, Sudheer, Ranjani, Nivi, Rajat, Aman and Simran; thanks, cheers and a big salute to my CSC and Satyam friends and all others who had donated their platelets for my last treatment. I owe a lot to you guys. No words can describe my gratitude for your kindness.

My list of friends is long and with my level of memory, I am sure I have missed a few important names; apologies to all of them.

Special thanks to my Engineering College (IERT) for giving hundreds of memorable moments that I rejoiced throughout my life.

I would like to thank all those who had given me even the smallest reason to smile. I even have a longer list since it's not a journey of writing a book, it's not book and papers, it's my life filled with emotions and moments.

Thanks to HCL and CSC for helping me financially for my last treatment.

Thanks to Aanchal Kanthaliya for your contribution in initial editing and being associated till the end. This book could not have been possible without you.

Thanks to Kanishka and his team at Writer's Side, for making it more presentable.

Thanks to Sristhi Publishers for offering an opportunity to voice out my story.

Thanks to Ankit Bhan and Udai Yadla for their contribution in the book.

Dear Friends, I apologize on my husband's behalf, if he has hurt anyone in any part of the book; he had no such intention. He had committed to me that the earning from the book will go for charity. I don't know how a miser like him accepted to do it.

Ajay had a crazy reason to write this book. He says, 'I want to make your memories immortal,' but I am sure I will remain alive in many hearts. I know my story had a sad ending, but don't look at the negative part of it. Life is a journey; we are born and we will reach the destination. This story was my voyage. It may be short, but meaningful. Just to tell you, I had two greatest desires in my life; one was to marry Ajay and second was to be blessed with a baby. I may not have been fortunate enough to be a mother, but I enjoyed my motherhood with Nanhu. Thanks Pooja di for gifting us with such a cute and lovely baby.

I am a lady with no regrets, no hard feelings and no enemies, but plenty of friends and a lovely family. What else could you ask from life? I can say with contention that I had travelled a quality journey that could be just a dream for billions.

I had only one reason behind this lengthy speech – please don't remember me as a tragedy queen. Remember me as a person who had lived less in number of years, but not in moments. And for all those who will do that, I would appreciate and say, 'love you; you are the best reader.'

Yours forever...

Bhavna

Her Last Wish

He was not a failure; he was just struggling to meet his father's expectations. A ray of hope walked into his life when he married her. She was smart, and a charismatic personality, who taught him to value himself. But destiny's cruel twist puts her in the way of death, with not much time to live.

He takes it upon himself to fight all odds – even his family if need be – to help her fight her medical condition. He decides to fight for her, with her.

Will a defeated son prove himself to be the best husband? Will he be able to change the course of fate?

Inspired from real life events, this is an inspiring story of love, relationships and sacrifice, which proves once again how a good wife makes the best husband.

About the author

Ajay K Pandey grew up in the modest NTPC township of Rihand Nagar with big dreams. He studied Engineering in Electronics at IERT (Allahabad) and MBA at IIMM (Pune) before taking up a job in a corporate firm. He is currently working with Cognizant, Pune. He grew up with a dream of becoming a teacher, but destiny landed him in the IT field.

Travelling, trekking and reading novels are his hobbies. Travelling to different places has taught him about different cultures and people, and makes him wonder how despite all the differences, there is a bond that unites them. Trekking always inspires him to deal with challenges like a sport. Reading is perhaps what makes him feel alive.

You are the Best Wife is his debut book based on his life events and lessons.

Apart from writing, he wants to follow his role model Mother Teresa, and make some contribution to the society. He aspires to start a charitable trust that would support aged people and educate special children.

After his debut book *You Are the Best Wife*, Ajay has authored bestselling titles *Her Last Wish* and *You Are the Best Friend*.

f : *AuthorAjayPandey*

: *@AjayPandey_08*

: *@author_ajaykpandey*

: *ajaypandey0807@gmail.com*

: *www.ajaykpandey.com*